The Trail of the Iron Horse

Walker A. Tompkins

Copyright © 1948 by Better Magazines, Inc.
Copyright © 1948 by Better Publications, Inc., renewed
Copyright © 1975 by C.B.S. Publications, The Consumer Publishing Division of C.B.S., Inc.
Copyright © renewed 1976 by Walker A. Tompkins

All rights reserved.

Published in 2005 by arrangement with
Golden West Literary Agency.

Wheeler Large Print Western.

The text of this Large Print edition is unabridged.
Other aspects of the book may vary from the original edition.

Set in 16 pt. Plantin by Carleen Stearns.

Printed in the United States on permanent paper.

Library of Congress Cataloging-in-Publication Data

Tompkins, Walker A.
    The trail of the iron horse / by Walker A. Tompkins.
      p. cm. — (Wheeler Publishing large print western)
    ISBN 1-58724-963-4 (lg. print : sc : alk. paper)
    1. Pacific railroads — Fiction. 2. Railroads — Design and construction — Fiction. 3. Outlaws — Fiction.
4. Large type books. I. Title. II. Wheeler large print western series.
PS3539.O3897T73 2005
    813'.54—dc22   2005001328

The Trail of
the Iron Horse

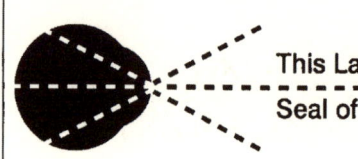
This Large Print Book carries the
Seal of Approval of N.A.V.H.

The Trail of
the Iron Horse

National Association for Visually Handicapped
serving the partially seeing

As the Founder/CEO of NAVH, the only national health agency solely devoted to those who, although not totally blind, have an eye disease which could lead to serious visual impairment, I am pleased to recognize Thorndike Press* as one of the leading publishers in the large print field.

Founded in 1954 in San Francisco to prepare large print textbooks for partially seeing children, NAVH became the pioneer and standard setting agency in the preparation of large type.

Today, those publishers who meet our standards carry the prestigious "Seal of Approval" indicating high quality large print. We are delighted that Thorndike Press is one of the publishers whose titles meet these standards. We are also pleased to recognize the significant contribution Thorndike Press is making in this important and growing field.

Lorraine H. Marchi, L.H.D.
Founder/CEO
NAVH

* Thorndike Press encompasses the following imprints: Thorndike, Wheeler, Walker and Large Print Press

CHAPTER I

Arrow and Saber

Throughout the bitter cold of the moonless Utah night, the Arapahoe war party had toiled on the steep south slope of Sundown Pass in the western foothills of the Wasatch Range, undermining the thousand-ton boulder perched five hundred feet above the Union Pacific tracks.

A copper-red dawn found the job in readiness. The warriors had time to relax in the concealment of the greasewood and sagebrush which mottled the canyon slope, eating their rations of pemmican and parched corn, drinking the water each brave carried in a plump buffalo-gut container.

The boulder was roughly spherical in shape, its tremendous mass weighing incalculable tons. Some prehistoric glacier had dropped the great granite chunk there. Union Pacific engineers, surveying the railroad through the Wasatch highlands, had inspected the poised boulder which, if it became dislodged, could crush a locomotive like a paper sack. They had concluded that nothing short of an earthquake could turn the boulder into a menace to life and property.

Twenty Arapahoe warriors had thought differently. They had undermined the hillside below the giant granite chunk until its center of gravity was a factor they could control by manipulating a pine-log lever on the uphill side. It had become a weapon which put the next passing train at the mercy of this handful of savages.

The waiting redskins regarded the rubble-ballasted roadbed of the U.P. as an enemy which would doom their tribe to extinction if it were not destroyed. The Arapahoe braves knew that the iron-tracked road had been approaching Utah for half a decade, across the buffalo-swarming plains of Nebraska, through Wyoming's Sioux-infested hills, into the barren desert of the Mormon country. But these shimmering steel rails had been laid too recently to have accumulated any rust from the scanty rainfall which April had brought to the Wasatches this spring of 1869.

The snorting "Iron Horses" which followed this thousand-mile trail toward the sunset would bring hosts of pale-faces to settle on the Indians' hunting ground. And it must be destroyed.

Directly below the suspended threat of the glacial boulder the railroad tracks were double, for this was the site of West Siding, where passenger trains cleared the main line to make way for the high-priority supply trains bringing rails and spikes and other supplies from Omaha, to feed the construction gangs which were pushing the Union Pacific steadily on toward the distant Pacific Ocean.

Daylight had hardly penetrated the deep chasm of Sundown Pass when the alert ears of the waiting Indians heard the faroff *whoom* of a locomotive whistle, pulled thin and wavering by the gusts of wind which brawled down the canyon. The rails were singing their sedative hum now, heralding the approach of an Iron Horse. Swiftly, the Arapahoe warriors slithered a reptilian passage out of the brush and assembled behind the poised boulder, ready to thrust their combined weight on the pine-log lever.

The deep-throated, gusty whistle of the locomotive which was approaching from the heat-shimmering floor of the western desert reached other ears than those of the Arapahoes. A hundred feet higher up the slope, following the narrow ledge trail which led to the side-track in the pit of the pass, two oddly contrasted riders moved over the shoulder of the mountain spur into the gorge.

One, a powerfully-built man in his middle twenties, wore the blue uniform of a cavalryman, and his line-back dun horse bore the scars of past skirmishes. He hipped around in his dusty McClellan saddle to address the flashily dressed Mexican youth who rode behind him on a magnificent black stallion.

"That'll be General Sherman's special, Celestino. We're making this rendezvous with less than five minutes to spare, looks like."

The handsome young Mexican's burnt-leather face revealed even white teeth in a grin, breaking through the fatigue of their hard overland trek from the Santa Fe country during the week past. His high-born lineage was evident in his aristocratic face.

"*Si*, General. It would not do to keep such an important man waiting, not when *El President* Grant himself ordered thees pow-wow een the Wasatches, *no es verdad?*"

It was obvious that Celestino's appellation of "General" was a nickname, for his partner's shoulder straps bore the double bars indicating a captain's rank.

This chestnut-haired, blue-eyed young soldier was none other than Captain Robert Pryor, a Texan who had enlisted with the Union cause at the outset of the Civil War. But, since his mustering out in '65, he had spent the intervening four years fighting a one-man war against the forces of oppression which were rampant in the frontier West.

That crusade had had its inception when Pryor, better known now in the Lone Star country as the "Rio Kid," had returned from the wars to find that his parents had been slain by renegades and his home laid waste. Shortly thereafter, the vengeance trail which he had taken at once had led him to the *hacienda* of the young Mexican who now was his constant companion in adventure, Celestino Mireles.

The Rio Kid had saved Mireles from a grisly death at the hands of outlaw raiders. As a result the two had formed a Damon and Pythias relationship which nothing short of death could sunder.

Bob Pryor continued wearing his cavalry

garb — flat-crowned campaign hat, yellow-striped breeches, spurred cavalry boots and Colt .45. But young Celestino dressed in the colorful *hidalgo* costume of his native south of the Border.

His steeple-crowned sombrero had ball tassels adorning its brim. His massive torso was covered by a tailored *gaucho* jacket of green velveteen trimmed with gold brocade. His *charro* pants were bell-bottomed, with vivid crimson velvet in the triangular seams. A cartridge bandolier slanted from shoulder to flank. His spike-heeled boots were of Hermosillo manufacture, and fitted with sunflower-roweled Spanish bits of ornate design.

"General," asked Celestino curiously, as he spurred his black alongside Pryor's mouse-colored dun, "*porque* would such great men as thos' General Sherman and Sheridan stop their train to veesit weeth us?"

The Rio Kid shrugged, reining up to squint off to the west. A feather of blue-black smoke was lifting above the lower foothills half a mile distant, indicating the approach of General Sherman's special east-bound train.

"You know as much as I do about this here business, Celestino," the Rio Kid commented. Although well educated, he always spoke in his native Texan idiom unless in the presence of celebrities. "These secret orders President Grant sent me in Santa Fe don't tell nothin' except that our presence here in the Wasatches — at least in Grant's opinion — is plumb important to the safety of the Union Pacific. Which is right flatterin' when yuh stop to think about it, *amigo*."

At that instant the locomotive snorted into view around a long curve down-grade, smoke belching from its funnel stack, its drive rods flashing in the sunlight. It was a short train, consisting of General Sherman's private coach, a car carrying a troop kitchen and bunks for the general's platoon of guards, and a box car for the soldiers' horses and supplies.

As the two riders watched from their lofty elevation at the crest of the pass, they saw the locomotive brake to a halt just west of the switch. A brakeman, looking like an ant from this height, swarmed out of the engine cab and ran forward to throw the switch, shunting the special onto West Siding.

"Come on," the Rio Kid grunted, inner excitement needling him. "We've got some steep sledding ahead of us before we get to the right-of-way down there and report for Sherman's orders. His party is prob'ly in a hurry to get back East."

Stirrup to stirrup, the two riders headed on down the ledge. The Union Pacific train, its bell setting up clanging echoes between the walls of the pass, chuffed slowly onto the sidetrack and halted directly below the trail they were descending.

"Celestino — look!"

Simultaneously with Pryor's sharp cry of warning, the Mexican's eagle-sharp eyes caught sight of what had brought the Rio Kid to a quick halt.

Directly below them, in a line with the halted train far below, a score or more of breech-clouted Indian warriors were swinging their weight on a pine-tree lever, teetering the vast ball-shaped granite boulder which hid them from the view of those on the train.

"Them Injuns are fixin' to roll that boulder onto General Sherman's train, 'Tino!" the Rio Kid shouted, hauling his Army Springfield .45-70 from its scabbard under his right saddle fender. "Come on — *andale!*"

A blood-curdling warwhoop went up from the knot of Indians behind the immense boulder below, as they caught sight of two horsemen spurring down the roof-steep slope above them, sunlight flashing on rifle barrels. A spate of gunshots bracketed the Rio Kid and Celestino with lead as the Indians dropped their log and whipped up muskets to fight off the unexpected attack on their rear.

Spurring their horses into a shallow defile which cut the slope, the Rio Kid and Celestino swarmed out of stirrups and up the gulch rim, rifles hammering their deathsong.

An Arapahoe wearing a six-foot-tailed war-bonnet threw up his hands, with a death scream, and rolled soddenly down the slope toward the railroad tracks far below. A sleet of arrows whined over the heads of the Rio Kid and Celestino as the paint-daubed bucks put their war bows into the action, plucking arrows from doeskin quivers slung behind their backs, each bow keeping two or more of the singing shafts in the air at the same time.

Laying their rifles aside, the Rio Kid and Celestino unholstered their six-guns. Braving the return fire, they aimed and triggered with precision, dropping their red-skinned targets into the rubble and brush of the mountainside.

Against ten-to-one odds, the two riders had the advantage of surprise and concealment. Then through the gun-smoke and dust, the Indians saw blue-coated soldiers piling out of the railroad car, sunlight bright on sabers and Springfields.

Facing the peril of being caught in a crossfire from above and below, the Arapahoes chose to retreat, racing off across the brushy slope toward a canyon where their war ponies were tethered in a bunch.

Dusty-faced, but grinning, the Rio Kid and Celestino Mireles swung astride their horses when the last of the retreating Arapahoes vanished over the skyline to eastward. The Indians, besides being thwarted in their scheme to destroy the train on the siding below, had left five of their number for buzzard bait on the precipitous slope of Sundown Pass.

CHAPTER II

Special Orders

The guns of General William Tecumseh Sherman's special troops covered the approach of Captain Bob Pryor and his Mexican partner as their horses zigzagged down the mountain slope to reach the level of the U.P. tracks. But there was no further sign of the thwarted Arapahoes. Defeated in their purpose to dislodge the great boulder, the redskins were fleeing for the refuge of the Wasatch uplands, minus the scalps they had hoped to glean from the palefaces aboard the Iron Horse.

Two officers wearing the stars of major generals stepped forward from the passenger coach as Pryor exchanged salutes with the lieutenant in charge of the cavalry platoon. They were the top-ranking leaders of America's post-war army — General Sherman and his second in command, General Philip Sheridan.

Both generals were grinning broadly as the Rio Kid rode up, dismounted, and turned his reins over to Celestino.

"Captain Robert Pryor, sir, reporting for special orders by command of President U. S. Grant."

Salutes dispensed with, Sherman and Sheridan shook hands with the Rio Kid while the members of their command stared in goggle-eyed astonishment at such a breach of military formality. They did not know that this handsome young stranger was an old friend of both their superior officers, having served under each as a scout in the Civil War.

"You kept your appointment promptly, Captain Pryor," Sherman said warmly, clapping the Rio Kid on the back.

The General, who had led the Union troops which had burned a forty-mile-wide swath from Atlanta to the sea during the Georgia campaign, lifted his field-glasses for another look at the big granite boulder up the slope. He had witnessed Pryor's brief skirmish there with the ambushed Indians.

"Lucky for us you did, Pryor," he commented. "That boulder would have smashed my coach like an eggshell. I must telegraph the U.P. engineers to dynamite that rock before it wrecks the main line."

After the Rio Kid had introduced Celestino Mireles to the two celebrated Union generals, Sherman escorted them inside his austerely appointed private railroad car. The engineer of the train, acting on orders from Sheridan's adjutant, moved the special fifty yards up the sidetrack, out from under potential danger from the boulder.

After passing cigars to his guests, General Sherman started pacing up and down the car, hands clasped behind his back. Then he began to speak.

"President Grant could not have sent me a man more competent to handle the business which brings you here, Captain Pryor," the highest-ranking Army officer in America said cordially. "You are doubtless curious as to why the President ordered you to meet us here in the Wasatches on our way back East?"

The Rio Kid, firing his cigar and savoring the rich smoke with obvious relish, sat at attention in the chair Sherman had offered him, and nodded courteously.

"Yes, sir. My secret orders, which reached me in Santa Fe ten days ago, gave no hint as to why I was put on this assignment. I reckon it has somethin' to do with the transcontinental railroad."

Sherman's lean, whiskery face was grave, as he nodded.

"As you know," he said solemnly, "my interest in the Union Pacific's linking the Atlantic and the Pacific Oceans is strictly military, not commercial. I feel that if the West is to be settled, a railroad is vital to that settlement. Until this railroad is completed, it would be impossible for the Army and Navy to defend a country three thousand miles broad."

The Rio Kid made no comment. He was aware that America's remote ocean shores would soon be connected by steel. The Union Pacific, financed by government subsidies and the ill-famed political graft machine called the Credit Mobilier, had been begun at Omaha, and was now nearing Great Salt Lake. At the same time, private financiers in California, including Governor Leland Stanford, Mark Hopkins, Collis P. Huntington and other celebrities, were building the Central Pacific eastward from the El Dorado country.

Both the U.P. and the C.P. were laying grades into Utah now. Rumor had it that the two lines would meet somewhere in the vicinity of Ogden within the next month or two, heralding the completion of one of America's most important national achievements.

"General Sheridan and I have just completed an inspection torn to end-of-track," Sherman continued, his face wreathed in cigar fumes. His eyes were slitted with a burning intensity which reminded the Rio Kid of the way Sherman had looked during the grim days of the Siege of Vicksburg, when the Kid had scouted for the Union commander some six years past.

"It has been no easy thing for our chief engineer, General Grenville Dodge, and his construction superintendent, General Jack Casement, to push their steel this far," admitted Sherman. "Financial trouble, Congressional red tape — they have been the least of our troubles. The Indians have seen their buffalo decimated by hunters supplying Casement's Irishmen with meat. They know the railroad will cut their hunting ground in two. They've fought us every mile of the way as the railroad has moved west, Captain Pryor. After saving our lives this morning from that Arapahoe band, you can see the nuisance these attacks have been."

Sherman halted his nervous pacing, gesturing at the Rio Kid with his long cigar.

"You'd think, Captain," he said gravely, "that our troubles were about over, now that Huntington's Chinese have pushed the Central Pacific out of California and Nevada and are nearing Salt Lake. My dream to have a railroad by which to transfer troops anywhere in the country in short order is about to come true. But we are facing forces of evil which are all the more dangerous because we can't be sure who or what they are. And that is why I asked the President to dispatch a trouble-shooter out here to help out."

The Rio Kid felt his pulses race. He felt honored, knowing that one of President Grant's first acts since becoming the occupant of the White House in Washington a month before had been to contact him, Bob Pryor, for this important mission.

"Here's the situation in brief." General Sheridan took up where his superior left off. "General Dodge is an engineer, loaned at Sherman's request from the U.S. Army to put this Union Pacific across the plains and deserts and mountains. Dodge has done a fine job, so far. But at every turn he is bucked by money-making crooks and high-placed politicians, who are becoming millionaires as a result of their contracts with the railroad."

The Rio Kid and Celestino exchanged glances, keeping discreetly silent. They had heard rumors of the multi-million-dollar stock manipulations of the Credit Mobilier, whose bankers in Boston and Manhattan were making a corrupt graft of the railroad.

"Now that the Central and the Union are approaching each other," Sheridan continued, "great pressure is being brought to bear by selfish interests upon both construction engineers — Dodge for the Union. Crocker of the C.P. Land promoters want the rails routed south of Great Salt Lake, which isn't feasible from an engineering standpoint. Brigham Young, naturally, wants the terminal to be in Salt Lake City, for the prestige it will bring his great Mormon capital."

Sherman cleared his throat, interrupting Sheridan.

"We mustn't convey the impression to the Rio Kid that a man of Brigham Young's caliber is corrupt," he warned. "Young is thoroughly honest, and one of America's truly great empire builders. His Latter-Day Saints converted a raw desert into a rose garden. But the petty grafters, land-grabbers out to fleece investors by selling them lots in non-existent cities along the right-of-way, are causing the trouble we face. The Mormons are not responsible in any way."

The Rio Kid was personally acquainted with Brigham Young and many other elders of the Tabernacle.

"I have only the greatest respect for the Saints," he said musingly.

Tersely, in crisp military phraseology, the two generals went on to explain that crooked contractors were trying to have both railroads cross the continent, since they made money for every mile of track that went down. Wasting taxpayers' money in extra mileage and unnecessary bridgework meant nothing to them.

"And now we come to my reason for wanting a trouble-shooter to do some intelligence work — call it spy duty, if you wish — in the Salt Lake area," General Sherman said, moving over in front of the Rio Kid and Celestino. "Word has come to me that a vast plot is taking shape which will not only jeopardize this transcontinental railroad, but which threatens the lives of the men in charge of its construction.

"Here, then," Sherman said earnestly, his hand on Pryor's knee, "are your confidential orders, Captain. Details of this plot are known to but one man — an Army Intelligence officer named Major Justin Ironwall. I shan't bore you with details, for

Major Ironwall will take care of that. As a matter of fact, the details have not been ironed out yet.

"You will contact Major Ironwall at the Sledge and Spike Hotel in Corinne, Utah, the hell-roaring town at end-of-track. Use President Grant's secret orders to identify yourself to Major Ironwall, who is going under an assumed name, and in mufti instead of uniform. Ironwall will identify himself to you by means of a finger ring he wears, in the shape of a golden dragon. Is that clear?"

Realizing that their interview was nearing an end, Captain Pryor got to his feet and saluted.

"Yes, sir. I'll leave for Corinne immediately, sir."

Sherman dragged a gold-braided sleeve across his perspiring, heavy-boned face.

"Ironwall is an elderly man, not physically capable of forcing a showdown with these individuals who are plotting against the Union Pacific and its builders," he said gravely. "I warn you, Captain Pryor, that if your mission becomes known, you yourself will be marked for death. As I notified President Grant back in Washington, the man he assigns to this mission is facing unknown dangers. It is perhaps a suicide mission. I want you to realize that, Captain Pryor, before you undertake to carry out these orders."

The Rio Kid squared his shoulders and grinned.

"Celestino and myself will do our best," he said.

Sherman and Sheridan shook hands with the two riders.

"I know that," the Army commander said, a smile breaking the taut reserve of his face. "The way you tackled those Indians up the canyon slope this morning would have convinced me that Grant sent us the right men, even if I hadn't known of your fine record under my command from Sixty-two to Sixty-four, Captain."

CHAPTER III

Death at End-of-track

From the Wasatches to end-of-track was a three-day trek on horseback, following the westward-pushing roadbed of the U.P.R. Dusk was flaming beyond the black crags of the Promontory Range north of Great Salt Lake when the Rio Kid and his Mexican partner gigged their hoof-sore mounts into the outskirts of Corinne.

One of the last of the brawling end-of-track towns, Corinne marked the sum total of wickedness and depravity which characterized similar boom camps along the thousand-mile extent of the overland railroad.

The lawlessness of such end-of-track towns as Julesburg, Cheyenne, Laramie and Evanston was already becoming popular in song and story, taking their place in American folk lore along with such wild cowboy capitals as Dodge City and Abilene. But these camps, and scores of other end-of-track towns which had bloomed and died overnight without taking permanent root, paled in comparison to the rowdy, bloody, brawling town that was Corinne, Utah, in April of Sixty-nine.

The Rio Kid and Celestino Mireles felt the impact of Corinne's unadulterated evil even as they entered the ugly outskirts of the place.

The Union Pacific tracks bisected the town. The false-front of saloons and honky-tonks, gambling halls and hurdy-gurdy houses bracketed the railroad, etched against the sunset like the uneven battlements of a ruined castle.

These board-and-bat deadfalls and honkies originally had been built back on the Nebraska prairies, but as end-of-track moved forward, their owners had dismantled the buildings and set them up again, preying on the lusty appetites and free-spending of the legions of Irish terriers who were building the U.P. west.

Less permanent were the canvas tents and the soddies where saloonmen dispensed watered whisky, and gamblers fleeced their customers through the medium of crooked roulette wheels, stacked decks, and loaded dice.

Off to the north were the machine shops and temporary roundhouses of the railroad. Sidetracks were occupied by seemingly endless rows of flat cars, loaded with cross ties and steel rails, barrels of spikes and crates of fishplates, supplies rushed out from the Eastern factories to keep the Irish spikers and graders, bridge-builders and tracklayers from being forced to halt operations through want of material.

But the railroad yards formed only a small, though vital, part of Corinne. The gamblers, painted women, bartenders and pickpockets who formed a westward-marching army paced by the advancing rails had taken over the town, preying on the construction gangs. It was in this section of town that the Rio Kid knew he would face the crux of the mystery which General Sherman had warned him about.

"*Caramba!*" muttered Celestino, spurring his black alongside the Rio Kid's dun. "When I was a *nino,* my *madre* read from her Bible of the wicked cities of Babylon, of Sodom an' Gomorrah. But thees town, General, she ees all thos' places rolled eento one, no? The *diablo* himself must dwell here."

The Rio Kid nodded, mentally comparing this end-of-track town with the wildest mining camps and Texas trail towns of his own experience. He agreed with Celestino's appraisal of Corinne. It was as if the devil had set up a part of Hades itself here on the bleak Utah desert, catering to the basest lusts and appetites known to mankind.

Their horses were working through the congested traffic of the main street now. The street was without sidewalks, a river of silver dust which rose high to choke their nostrils and impede their vision.

The offscourings of humanity were gathered here. Gamblers in frock coats and Jezebels in crinoline were taking their sundown promenade before the night's work began. Buckskin-clad mountaineers, hunters and trappers; bearded Mormons and blanket-clad Indians; tenderfeet fresh off the train from Missouri and Illinois and New Jersey. All rubbed shoulders in a polyglot tide of humanity unparalleled in the world's history.

Barkers took their places in front of saloons where kerosene flares guttered in the twilight, shouting the attractions of their establishments:

"Come on, you rondo-coolo sports! Our bar serves the finest rotgut in the West. Give our games a try! Get an honest deal!"

Work trains, fresh from the far end of

track west of town, were rolling into Corinne, discharging their Irish crews, adding to the weltering confusion of the place. Burly spikers and graders, sweat-stained from a hard day's toil under the Utah sun, jostled in converging streams as they headed for bars and poker tables.

For all its depravity and confusion, Corinne's spirit laid its sharp edge against the Rio Kid, quickening his heart with a sense of danger and adventure. Spurring his dun horse, Saber, against the flow of traffic, hand poised close to the butt of his holstered Dragoon he drank in the myriad smells and sounds and sights of Corinne. He sensed its underlying drama, its cross-currents of greed and jealousy and hate and sham love.

They despaired of finding hitching space at the tie-racks which fronted the main street buildings. Their ears rang from the din of sound — saloon barkers, the blare of a brass band from the Red Tent Dance Hall, the shrill laughter of women.

A U.P. work engine snorted over by the yards. Somewhere a blacksmith's sledge rang on an anvil. A burst of gunshots breached the pandemonium with louder, flatter cacophony.

Then they caught sight of their destination — a block-long building with an unpainted false front and canvas circus-tent roof. Tar torches illuminated a sign painted above a wooden awning which made a series of sway-backed scallops along the crowded porch:

SLEDGE & SPIKE HOTEL

Reining toward the hotel to avoid a string of tandem-hitched freight wagons up from Salt Lake and Ogden with a cargo of barreled whisky for the Corinne deadfalls, the Rio Kid and Celestino dismounted. They searched in vain for an empty spot at the hotel's hitchrack.

"Wait here, *amigo*," Bob Pryor said, passing Saber's reins to his Mexican *compañero*. "I'll see if I can locate Major Ironwall before we hunt up a place to eat supper."

Celestino scowled, fingering his gun butt absently.

"Take care, General," the Mexican warned. "There are men een thees misbegotten *cuidad* who would slit your t'roat for a wooden *peso*. I weesh we deed not have to be separated."

Pryor mopped his face with his bandanna neckerchief, swatting the alkali dust of their long trail off his blue cavalry tunic.

"Nobody knows why we've come to end-of-track," he pointed out.

Leaving Celestino with his somber doubts, the Rio Kid climbed the porch steps and approached a pair of hooked-open batwing doors. Pausing in clotted shadow, he checked the loads in his Dragoon six-shooter, loosening the gun in its scabbard before entering the Sledge & Spike.

The entire lower floor of the hostelry was given over to a barroom and gambling hall. The fetid odors of tobacco smoke, cheap whisky, perfume and sweating human flesh assailed his nostrils in sickening waves.

The long pine bar, scarred from its froghopping course across Nebraska and Wyoming and Utah, was jammed with Irish terriers, Eastern tenderfeet, miners, and businessmen. Percentage girls, lured by the Rio Kid's rugged good looks, solicited his trade a dozen times before he had worked his way to the foot of a staircase leading to the upper story.

A sleepy-faced clerk was on duty at a packing-case desk which the Rio Kid identified as the hotel's headquarters by the key rack nailed to a post behind him. The clerk eyed him indifferently as the Rio Kid approached, his face sharp-etched in the glow of ceiling lamps.

"Room will be ten bucks a night — in advance," grunted the clerk, shoving a dog-eared register toward Pryor.

Pryor grinned, dropping a gold octagonal in the clerk's palm.

"I'm looking for a customer of yours, man named Jesse Pickett, of Kirksville, Missouri."

The clerk pocketed the gold piece, thumbed through the hotel register and glanced up.

"Room JJ," he said. "Top of the stairs and turn left. And don't try to bed down with Pickett, feller. Extry guest is charged six bucks a night."

The Rio Kid gave the clerk his assurance he would not try anything of the sort, and mounted the stairway, holding his breath against the milky layers of smoke which billowed around the ceiling level. The hubbub of the barroom died in his ears as he turned left down a long, murky corridor flanked by closely-spaced doors.

"Jesse Pickett" was the assumed name which the Army spy, Major Ironwall, had adopted for his incognito role here in Corinne, General Sherman had told the Rio Kid.

★ ★ ★

Reaching a flimsy door marked "JJ", the Rio Kid knocked. He got no answer, but, seeing a bar of lamplight under the door, he tested the knob and found the door unlocked.

Stepping inside, the Rio Kid found the canvas-walled cubicle furnished only with a narrow cot, ventilated by a single grimy window. A whale-oil lamp flickered in a wall sconce above the door.

"Major Ironwall?"

The Rio Kid addressed his question to a man who lay on the cot, apparently asleep. He was a man in his sixties, with iron-gray Dundrearie whiskers bracketing his thin face.

Receiving no answer, the Rio Kid stepped over to the bed and leaned down, intending to shake Ironwall awake. Then it was that he saw the stab wound in Ironwall's scrawny chest, saw the pool of blood which soaked the dead man's shirt front.

Major Ironwall's body was still warm. He had been killed only a short time before!

Pryor confirmed that the death of Justin Ironwall had been recent when he saw that the man's lifeblood was still welling from the knife wound over his heart, the guttering stream not yet having had time to drip down on the blanket over the cot.

Death had visited Room JJ in the Sledge & Spike Hotel directly ahead of the Rio Kid, then. In spite of Ironwall's efforts to keep his spy work a secret here at end-of-track, the Intelligence officer had paid the penalty which his dangerous job involved.

Obviously Ironwall had died in his sleep, for the room showed no signs of a struggle. A six-gun was in a holster at Ironwall's thigh. But the pockets of his butternut trousers and those of his broadcloth shirt had been turned wrong-side out by his slayer.

The ruffled condition of the pillow under the dead man's head told Pryor that something had been pulled out from under it. Stooping to peer under the cot, the Rio Kid located Ironwall's only baggage — a carpet-bag with a padlock snapped over its leather handles.

A knife blade — the death weapon, judging from the bloodstains on the carpet-bag — had been used to slash open the bag. It was empty. Whatever papers or other secret material Ironwall had carried in the bag and kept under his pillow for safekeeping were now in the hands of his unknown slayer.

Pryor went to the window, peering out across a jumble of canvas roofs marking the buildings of Corinne's redlight district. Justin Ironwall's killing was a severe blow to his own plans, for the key to the whole situation here at end-of-track was locked in the dead man's brain. Whatever information Ironwall had assembled during his months with the Union Pacific was now gone beyond recall. Within minutes of the time when Bob Pryor would have arrived to take over Ironwall's responsibilities, death had struck the elderly Army officer.

Then a random thought struck Pryor, relaxing the sharp tension that pulled at his nerves. What if this dead man wasn't Major Justin Ironwall? What if the hotel clerk downstairs had misread the register?

Ironwall could be identified by a gold dragon finger ring, General Sherman had said. Perhaps this corpse in Room JJ was some poor unfortunate who had been killed and robbed by some prowling footpad who preyed on drunken or sleeping inmates of the hostelry.

The Rio Kid turned, with the intention of inspecting the dead man's hands. And in so doing he was brought up short by the sudden opening of the corridor door.

A heavy-set man on whose vest gleamed

a marshal's badge was framed there, one craggy hand holding the Rio Kid under the menace of a Confederate Spiller & Burr five-shot revolver.

"Lift 'em, stranger!" the Corinne lawman bit out, jerking his gaze off the dead man on the cot. "This is the third customer in two weeks who's been knifed in this hotel!"

CHAPTER IV

Jail on Wheels

As the Rio Kid jerked his arms to hatbrim level, thoughts spun through his head. It would not do to identify himself, and tell his reason for being in Ironwall's room. He had heard of the corrupt officials in these railroad camps, and had no way of knowing whether this gun-toting star man was reliable or not.

With swift skill, the marshal jerked the Rio Kid's Dragoon .45 from leather and thrust it into the baggy pocket of his coat. In frisking Pryor's tunic for concealed weapons, he drew out the red-boarded envelope containing President Grant's secret orders, the Rio Kid's only identification.

"Hold on, hombre!" Pryor cried in desperation. "You can't take that!"

The marshal's Spiller & Burr clicked ominously as he backed off. Opening the envelope with his teeth, he whipped open the official document.

"Robert Pryor . . . special duty U.S.

Army," the lawman read musingly. "Well, Cap'n, yore wearin' a uniform don't excuse yuh killin' folks in their beds when yuh're off duty. I'm Tom Shelly, Marshal of Corinne. I reckon I'm goin' to clap yuh into jail till Gen'l Dodge figgers out what to do with yuh. He handles the punishment of military folks in these parts."

The Rio Kid breathed easier, realizing that the U.P.'s chief engineer, General Dodge, would speedily extricate him from this dilemma. It made it unnecessary for him to give this marshal any further information.

"Pore ol' Jesse Pickett," grunted Marshal Shelly, staring down at the dead man. "Played many a round of poker with him over at the Big Tent. Only square gambler in town."

Shelly produced a pair of handcuffs and snapped them over the Rio Kid's wrists. Leaving Room JJ, they headed down the hall, passed hotel guests who stared curiously from their doorways as Shelly reamed his long-barreled gun into Pryor's back.

One thing, at least, Bob Pryor knew. The dead man, masquerading as Jesse Pickett, undoubtedly had been Major Justin Ironwall. His death would be serious news to General Dodge.

Out on the street, Celestino Mireles was shaping himself a cigarette when he caught sight of the Rio Kid being ushered out of the hotel by a gun-toting lawman. But so inured to such sights were the people of Corinne that they gave the marshal and his handcuffed prisoner only a passing notice.

Mireles stood transfixed in the act of cementing his quirly with his tongue. The Rio Kid had run afoul of some kind of trouble with the local law! On the other hand, it was impossible to go to Pryor and question him. Their relationship was a secret they must keep inviolate.

Ground-tying Saber and his own black stallion, the Mexican youth moved off through the shadows, following the Rio Kid at a ten-yard distance. He saw the lawman escort the Kid across the crowded street and down an alley between a dance hall and a land office, in the direction of the Union Pacific yards.

Trailing them down the alley, Celestino kept to the shadows. He saw the Rio Kid hustled around the end of a troop train loaded with Army personnel, and on to a short spur track where a lone box car was standing.

An elusive shadow against the night's blackness, Celestino skirted the Army train. He saw that a ramp led to the open door of the box car. The headlight of a switch engine on a turntable two blocks down the tracks swept its yellow cone across the lone car, and Celestino saw that it was fitted with iron-barred windows.

This car, then, was a jail on wheels. It was probably Corinne's calaboose, a portable bastille which moved from camp to camp.

A few minutes later the marshal emerged from the jail car, trundled its door shut and snapped a massive padlock.

Celestino Mireles, his unfired cigarette drooping from his lips, had a moment of indecision. He could wait until the marshal left, then slip up to the jail car and have a talk with the Rio Kid. But instinct warned the Mexican to tail the lawman. He could always return to the jail car for a pow-wow with his partner. But once Pryor's captor lost himself in Corinne's crowded streets, he might be hard to find.

Marshal Shelly left the railroad yards at a trot and headed up the alley toward the main street. Celestino was five yards behind him when Shelly turned right and hammered on the door of a tin-roofed shanty whose lamplighted windows revealed a sign:

OVERLAND ENTERPRISES
CRADE FALK, PROP.
REAL ESTATE
Bought Sold Traded

Celestino Mireles was an obscure shadow lounging against the corner of Crade's land office when the door opened and a big man in a top hat and fustian steelpen coat stepped out to confront the marshal. Shelly's agitated words did not reach Mireles, but the Mexican's heart pounded violently against his ribs when he saw the marshal hand the speculator a familiar red-bordered envelope. The Rio Kid's secret orders from President U. S. Grant!

"What next, Falk?" the marshal asked loud enough for Celestino to hear. "The man's a soldier. Gen'l Dodge's jurisdiction, not mine."

Crade Falk tugged at his cinnamon-red rams-horn mustaches, rolling a stogie in his harsh lips. His gooseberry-green eyes scanned President Grant's document swiftly, and Celestino saw the land promoter's jaw take on a hard angle against the lamplight which silhouetted him.

"Pryor," he said unpleasantly. "That'll be the Rio Kid. This is bad medicine,

Tom. Reckon this calls for Rickaree's special talents."

Closing and locking the door of his office, Crade Falk headed up the street, the marshal matching his stride. Celestino moved after them, saw the pair quarter across the street and enter the doors of the Red Tent Casino.

By the time Celestino could reach the doorway, he had lost track of the black-coated marshal. A moment's swift survey of the crowded gambling hall, however, revealed the tall figure of Falk standing at a blackjack table, whispering to one of the players.

Celestino faded back against the wall by the front door as he saw the blackjack player cash in his chips. Nodding in response to Crade Falk's instructions, he hitched up his gun-belt and headed for the door.

The gambler was a smallpox-scarred half-breed whose Indian blood was apparent at first glance. This, then, would be Rickaree, whose "special talents" were not hard to guess. Crade Falk was enlisting the help of a professional gunhawk!

Rickaree passed Celestino at arm's length and headed out into the night, a cold grin on his lips. Celestino, glancing around before following Rickaree on his mission, saw Crade Falk moving in the direction of the roulette layout, shaking hands with the sallow-faced croupier there. Then Celestino slipped out of the place.

He had no difficulty in trailing Falk's gunman. Rickaree was making a beeline toward the Union Pacific tracks and the jail car where the Rio Kid was being held prisoner.

Made reckless by a sense of danger heading Bob Pryor's way, Celestino matched Rickaree's running gait. He almost lost the gunhawk when the troop train started moving down the tracks, and had to sprint hard to skirt the chuffing locomotive.

He leaped the tracks in time to see Rickaree's bulky figure mounting the cleated ramp to the door of the jail car. Celestino moved stealthily across the right-of-way, his boots making a soft abrasive sound on the clinkers, and with urgency crowding him hard.

The half-breed unlocked the jail door, using a key which the marshal must have turned over to Crade Falk. The door trundled open and Rickaree stepped into the car.

A lantern revealed the two cells which

partitioned off one end of the jail car, a barrier of latticed strap iron. Standing in the locked door of the left-hand cell was the blue-clad figure of the Rio Kid.

"What's up, hombre?" Pryor demanded, clubbing his fists over the iron straps. "Are you from General Dodge?"

Rickaree's swarthy face was a satanic mask in the glare of the ceiling lantern. Gun metal made a rasping sound as Rickaree pulled a .41 derringer from a concealed holster under his shirt, aiming the stubby barrel at the Rio Kid's chest.

"I'm here to cash in yore chips, soldier!" Rickaree chuckled hoarsely, moving up closer. "Yuh've stuck yore horns into somethin' too big for yuh."

The Rio Kid fell back from the gunhawk's derringer, knowing that the barrier of the cell's door offered scant protection from the bullet in the breed's gun. He saw Rickaree's trigger finger whiten at the knuckle, saw the cold glints in the man's eyes which told of the cruel streak of sadism which was the hallmark of a fiend to whom killing was a pleasure.

Pryor's body quivered, awaiting the expected slam of point-blank lead tunneling his chest. Then the wick of the lantern in the jail car jumped to the concussion of a gunshot.

But it was not Rickaree's .41 hideout gun which had exploded. From the open door of the jail car the muzzle flash of a Colt spewed its fiery lance out of the night.

Slack-jawed in amazement, the Rio Kid saw the half-breed spin around under the impact of a slug which smashed the derringer from his lead-ruined fist. Slick with bullet shock, Rickaree sagged to his knees, jerking his head around to face the doorway.

"Celestino!"

Pryor yelled the name joyously, as he saw the welcome features of his Mexican partner limned in the lantern light. Celestino Mireles vaulted to the ramp and came into the car, his leveled Colt trailing a rope of gunpowder smoke.

With a hoarse bawl of fear, the half-breed gunman pawed in his hip pocket with his left hand. Lanternlight flashed off the barrel of another derringer. And with only a shaved instant to spare, Celestino tripped his gun-hammer a second time. His second shot smashed Rickaree in the chest, driving the half-breed to the floor, his derringer blasting in his fist to rip a splintered furrow across the planking.

Celestino moved in fast then, staring down at Rickaree. The half-breed was dying, for a slug had lodged close to his heart. Rickaree's boots drummed the floor planks in a grisly tattoo as paroxysms of agony shot through him.

"You're heading for blazes, senor!" Celestino rasped, leaning over the dying killer. "You die because you work for Senor Crade Falk, no? Why do you do thees?"

Rickaree's head rolled on the floor, his pain-brightened eyes peering through the cell door at the Rio Kid. The semblance of a grin plucked at the breed's mouth, and crimson foam was forming at the corners of his lips.

"Falk — ransom for Gen'l Dodge," panted the outlaw. "Got — nothin' personal ag'in yuh — Rio Kid. Followin' — orders . . ."

Rickaree's eyes rolled in their sockets, and life was extinct when the Mexican holstered his gun and turned to face Pryor.

"What ees thees, General?" Celestino demanded, reaching through the bars to grip his partner's hand. "What does thees *mestizo* mean when he makes *habla* about a ransom for *El General* Dodge?"

The Rio Kid shrugged. Quickly he informed Celestino of his discovery of Ironwall's murder and his subsequent arrest. Celestino provided the details of Marshal Tom Shelly's visit to the speculator, Crade Falk, and Rickaree's killer mission.

"I've got to get out of this *juzgado* fast, Celestino," the Rio Kid said desperately, shaking the heavy steel door. "That doublecrossing marshal will be around to check on this breed's work before long. See if Rickaree's got the cell key in his pocket. He unlocked the outside padlock easily enough."

A quick examination of the dead man's pockets revealed but one key, that which had opened the outside padlock.

"This lock's too beeg for me to shoot open," Celestino said. Nervous sweat was dewing his swarthy forehead. "But eet ees plain to see that we have tangled weeth the *cabrones* that General Sherman weeshes us to destroy, *si!*"

CHAPTER V

Commandeered Engine

Knowing that time was fast running out for them, that any moment might see Tom Shelly and perhaps Crade Falk visiting the jail car to make sure that the Rio Kid had been disposed of, the two partners fell into a taut silence. The Rio Kid's identity was no longer a secret. General Grant's orders reposed in Crade Falk's pocket at this moment. Pryor's connection with the Intelligence officer, Justin Ironwall, who had been killed would be easy enough to deduce.

Celestino snapped his fingers as an idea came to him.

"I come back *pronto*, General," he said. "Take my gon."

Thrusting his Colt butt-foremost through the cell door, the Mexican vanished down the jail car ramp. Fifty yards away was a big sheet-iron building which Celestino recognized as a U.P. repair shop. Workmen were busy inside, hoisting the boiler off a defective locomotive as Celestino entered the shop.

Emboldened by his urgency, Celestino stepped over to a workbench racked with a wide variety of tools. When he made his exit a moment later, unnoticed by the wipers and mechanics in the engine pits, he carried a heavy hacksaw and a packet of extra blades under his *gaucho* jacket.

Back in the jail car, he handed the hacksaw though the bars to the Rio Kid with a brusque:

"Get to work, General. I have a plan."

Before the Rio Kid could ask any questions, Celestino was gone. Further up the siding which the jail car occupied, he had seen a work engine taking on water at a big tank. That locomotive was of prime importance to the scheme which had bloomed full-grown in Celestino's fertile brain.

Sprinting up the tracks, past the panting boiler of the switch engine, Celestino pushed through the steam jets which hissed from the cylinder cocks of the six-wheeler. Seizing a cabin grab-rail, he hoisted himself up the iron steps.

A roundhouse man who had just finished with the water tank spout was climbing down into the engine cab from the tender. He started at Celestino in surprise.

"Senor," Celestino said gruffly, "theese locomotive has work to do tonight. I am —"

"Yuh're drunk. Get off before I throw yuh off."

"Senor," Celestino said grimly, "I want you to hook onto a box car, *sabe usted?*"

The railroad man grinned tolerantly, believing he was facing a drunken Mexican bent on having some fun.

"Sober up, friend," he advised. "This loco is headed for the roundhouse for oilin'. I got no time to waste."

Something in the grim set of Celestino's jaws made the young U.P. hoghead pause in the act of reaching for the Johnson bar.

"You *sabe* how to wrangle thees Iron Horse, *amigo?*" asked Mireles.

"Shore, but what's that got to do with it?"

Celestino's other six-gun flashed into the open then, its hammer eared back to full cock.

"Hook onto that calaboose car up the tracks, *amigo!*"

The hoghead gulped, automatically shoving the Johnson bar into reverse. His hand trembled as he reached for the throttle lever.

"Yuh're crazy, tryin' to get away with this stunt, son," he growled. "That's Marshal

Tom Shelly's jail, that box car."

Celestino clicked his gunhammer ominously.

"Eef that car ees not five miles out of Corinne eenside of ten minutes, Senor, you weel be a dead man."

The railroader shuddered, opening the throttle a notch. The big drivers rolled, easing the work engine down-tracks toward the jail car. Leaning out the cab window, the hoghead scanned the right-of-way desperately. But there was no help closer than the grease monkeys and engine wipers in the nearby shops. The regular engineer of this loco was at supper, over in General Dodge's mess car.

A moment later the couplers thundered together and draw-bars grated metallically, as the locomotive hammered against the jail car.

Shaking with fear, the hoghead adjusted his Johnson bar, eased the brakes, and fed steam to the pistons. Seated on the fireman's bench across the cab, his face grim in the ruddy flicker of the open firebox, Celestino kept the railroader under his gun drop.

Slowly the engine gathered speed, rolling backward and pulling the car along, passing the dark bulk of the water tank and clattering over the main line switch points. Celestino had leaned his spine against the window frame and was drawing in his first relaxed breath in an hour — when a bullet punched through the window beside the boiler head and whipped the air an inch from the Mexican's nose.

Flinging himself to the iron floor of the cab, Celestino scuttled to the cab door and thrust his head out. Marshal Tom Shelly was racing up the tracks in hot pursuit, flame spitting from his revolver.

A bullet caromed off the funnel stack of the locomotive, another punched a slot in the boiler jacket by the safety valve dome. Then they were out of range. Getting to his feet, Celestino turned to order the engineer to increase speed.

But his voice died in his throat. The hoghead, seizing advantage of his opportunity, had leaped out of the cab.

Celestino pouched his Colt and sprang to the engineer's window to peer out. He saw the hoghead sprawled on the right-of-way, with Marshal Shelly slogging up to assist him to his feet.

Running the Iron Horse and, just as important, bringing it eventually to a stop, was now Celestino's problem!

A railroad engine was completely foreign

to Celestino's experience, but out of the maze of gauges and valves and levers on the boiler head, he recognized the throttle bar. Reaching for it, he jerked the lever a couple of notches on its quadrant.

Unfamiliar with the tremendous latent power of a steam engine, Celestino hastily eased off the throttle when he felt the locomotive shudder violently as the drive wheels, responding to the sudden jet of steam in the cylinders, began to spin on the rails without getting traction. Sparks showered into the night, the drive rods threshing impotently.

But under the eased-off throttle, the thunder of the exhaust settled to a rhythmic chuffing beat. Not knowing how to feed sand to the rails from the storage dome on the roof of the boiler, Celestino had to let the locomotive pick up its own traction, and in doing so automatically pick up speed.

The Mexican youth was sweating profusely as the work engine rumbled over the Bear River trestle east of town and settled down to a jouncing mile-a-minute clip, eastbound on the arrow-straight main line toward the Wasatch Range, remote on the horizon.

Reaction had set in after the strain of the

past hour. Celestino knew that the Rio Kid would be working frantically with the hacksaw, back in the jail car. He also knew that Marshal Tom Shelly would give the alarm back in Corinne. He would have no difficulty in rounding up a posse of soldiers from the garrison which occupied the tent camp there. And the Union Pacific yard superintendent would gladly loan Shelly the use of a locomotive to pursue the stolen engine and jail car.

Watching the fresh yellow poles of the telegraph line flash by the cab windows as the tracks curved southward toward Ogden, another disturbing possibility occurred to Celestino. News of the runaway engine would be flashed ahead, not only to clear the main line of possible traffic, but to have a posse waiting to arrest the man who had stolen the engine.

The green eyes of sidetrack switches blurred past. But to the south, below the black corrugated ridges through which the tracks knifed their way in a series of compound curves and cuts and fills, Celestino caught the glow of Brigham Station five miles away.

The red eye of an open switch loomed against the ebon back-drop of a hill a mile ahead. Celestino had no intention of derailing the rolling stock he had commandeered in this emergency. He had enough native savvy to realize that that red lantern signified danger.

Accordingly, he turned his attention once more to the bewildering array of levers on the boiler head. He rammed the throttle home, felt the locomotive slow down. It was gradually losing its head of steam anyway, but the Mexican youth realized that momentum might coast the engine the remaining distance to Brigham Station. And without doubt danger awaited him and the Rio Kid there.

He tested various levers without finding the brake mechanism. Pulling the Johnson bar into neutral seemed to add to the speed of the idling locomotive.

Taking a chance, he thrust the Johnson bar into reverse position. Drivers screamed their protest on the rails. The locomotive cab vibrated like a ship in a heavy sea.

Then, quite by accident, he found the brake lever and locked shoes against the drivers. The locomotive grated to a halt after a fifty-yard skid which sent out a metallic shriek which Celestino was positive must have reached Shelly's ears in Corinne.

Dropping out of the cab, with the hot,

panting breath of the locomotive boiler in his ears, Celestino sprinted back to the jail car and scrambled inside. The ceiling lantern was swinging like a pendulum in its bracket overhead.

The Rio Kid's hacksaw ceased its abrasive rasp as Celestino stepped over to the cell door, noting with approval that his partner had made the most of his time during their mad dash across the desert floor. The padlock hasp was sawed nearly a quarter of the way through.

"As an engineer, yuh'll make a good bronc-buster, *amigo!*" the Rio Kid panted hoarsely. A livid bruise was on his left cheekbone where he had been thrown violently against the iron lattice. "I been rattlin' around in this cell like a pair of dice in a chuck-a-luck cage."

Celestino grinned ruefully.

"Your arms are tired, General. Hand me the saw."

The Rio Kid had worn out the blade, and Celestino worked swiftly to install a new one from the packet he had filched from the U.P. machine shop.

Jaw locked grimly, the Mexican fitted the saw blade in the shallow kerf which the Rio Kid had already cut into the metal hasp, and resumed work. Metal dust glittered in the lamplight as the tempered blade bit deeper and deeper. The Rio Kid flexed his arm muscles and rested until he saw Celestino beginning to tire.

In the moment's silence when the saw was exchanged, with the Rio Kid thrusting his right arm through the latticed opening, their ears caught a faint humming sound in the rails outside. An infinitesimal vibration was transmitted through the jail car's trucks to their boot soles.

"Train comin'," the Rio Kid said grimly. "Shelly's wolf pack didn't waste much time givin' chase."

Celestino, mopping his damp face with a sleeve, stepped to the car door and leaned out.

To the northwest, from the direction of Corinne, a locomotive headlight stabbed the darkness, five miles away, but coming fast. The Rio Kid's escape depended on how much sawing they could do in the next five or six minutes at the most.

Pryor manipulated the hacksaw until his arm, cramped in the narrow opening of the cell door, wilted completely. Celestino snatched the tool from his hand and carried on the job, with hardly the loss of a stroke.

The humming of the rails increased in

volume. The Corinne marshal's locomotive was out of the hills now, and bearing down on the jail car and its attached engine. The headlight beam threw greasewood and boulders along the right-of-way into sharp relief.

"Eet ees ready, General!" Celestino Mireles said.

CHAPTER VI

Desert Flight

Celestino flung the hacksaw aside as the hasp was severed. Stooping over to the body of Rickaree, the Mexican pried the derringer from the dead outlaw's locked fingers and, using the stubby .41 barrel for a pry, forced the opening in the hasp.

With shaking fingers the Rio Kid clawed the huge padlock through the gap in the hasp. The next moment he was stepping out of the cell.

They leaped to the car door and saw the blinding yellow eye of the oncoming locomotive bearing down the tracks at slackening speed. An intervening tangent swung the headlight's beam slightly to the south, putting the jail car doorway in momentary shadow.

Seizing the opportunity to leap out of the car without being seen by the men in the oncoming locomotive, the Rio Kid and Celestino dropped to the ground. They raced up alongside the locomotive and around its front end.

They halted in front of the long plow-shaped cowcatcher, crouching in the shadow of the engine as Shelly's locomotive ground to a steam-hissing halt a few yards uptrack from the rear end of the jail car.

The funneling shadow of the jail car blackened the adjacent right-of-way now, and the two fugitives left the track and flung themselves into the dense sagebrush which encroached on the edge of the right-of-way.

Twenty yards back in the brush, they hunkered down and waited, peering through the foliage toward the two locomotives.

Men were swarming out of the cab of the pursuing engine, converging on both sides of the jail car. The fugitives heard Marshal Tom Shelly's shouted curse as the Corinne lawman clambered into the jail car and spotted the corpse there.

"They plugged Rickaree, gents!"

"Danged if they didn't have a hacksaw, Marshal," another voice rumbled inside the car. "With the U.P. iron on the handle. This was stole from our shops!"

Confusion inside the jail car died off momentarily as Shelly's yell knifed through the darkness.

"They can't be far, men! This hasp is still hot from bein' sawed! Hicks, you take the south side of the tracks. Ferryman, you an' me will scout the north side."

The Rio Kid and Celestino checked their six-gun cylinders. They were crouched in the brush on the north side of the roadbed, and dared not make a move. Any attempt to slither off through the sage would betray them to the Corinne star-toter.

"Marshal," came the protesting voice of one of the men — Celestino recognized it as that of the young Irishman whose locomotive he had commandeered — "I know for a fact that Mexican is armed! Chasin' outlaws in the dark ain't any affair of mine."

The Rio Kid and Mireles grinned in the darkness as they heard Shelly's profane arguing.

"Dang it to blazes, men, I'm *orderin'* yuh to help hunt them curly lobos down! This Rio Kid jasper killed Jesse Pickett over at the hotel which was why I jailed him. The Mexican must have shot Rickaree."

"What was Rickaree doin' in the jail car?" demanded the Irish railroader. "Didn't yez lock it?"

The Rio Kid chuckled. "That'll be a hard one for Shelly to answer, I reckon," he whispered. "He'll pull in his horns pronto."

In a moment or so they saw Tom Shelly round the back end of the jail car, peering out across the sage flats toward where the Rio Kid and his partner were hiding. Indecision was in the marshal's bearing now. Tracking down an armed foe, men who would be desperate if cornered, was no job to be performed on a moonless night.

Shelly shrugged and turned back to the men whose legs were visible between the trucks of the jail car.

"Hicks, fetch that engine of yores back to the Corinne yards," the marshal ordered. "I'll roust out a posse over here when it gets daylight and see if I can pick up their sign. There's no use riskin' an ambush tonight."

Five minutes later the two locomotives, one in reverse, were heading toward Corinne, the jail car sandwiched between them.

"What now, General?" Celestino asked wearily, as they got to their feet in the waist-high brush.

The Rio Kid's eyes were on the glow of the horizon marking the location of Corinne.

"Back to town," he growled grimly, "to

dab our loop on this Crade Falk hombre. I got a hunch that skunk knows the answers to the questions we would have asked Major Ironwall . . ."

Midnight saw the two fugitives limp into Corinne's blaze of lights. They had walked the railroad ties out of the desert, both because the U.P. route was the shortest, and because the ballasted roadbed left no sign for Tom Shelly's posse to cut the next day.

But eight miles in high-heeled cowboots was sheer torture to men whose feet were meant for stirrups.

Hunger made its insistent demands on them, and the tantalizing odors of coffee and sizzling steaks in the restaurants they passed were a well-nigh irresistible invitation. But the Rio Kid pulled in his belt another notch and slogged grimly on.

"The marshal's had time to tell Crade Falk that his little killer scheme ran afoul of a snag — thanks to you, Celestino," the Rio Kid said as they were neared the center of town. "Falk will be mighty desperate. But we have one advantage. He hasn't seen either one of us."

Celestino Mireles, hobbling painfully on blistered feet, pointed out the location of Crade Falk's land office a block further up the street. Its windows were yellow squares of lamplight, indicating that Falk did a "land-office business" even in the middle of the night.

"What do you plan to do weeth Senor Falk, General?" Celestino demanded curiously. "He may go for hees gons when you force a showdown, and eet ees important we capture the *cabrone* alive, eef we are to fin' out what happened to Major Ironwall, no?"

Bob Pryor laughed harshly. Despite his fatigue, he was in fine fettle for the imminent meeting with the speculator.

"I keep harkin' back to what that halfbreed, Rickaree, said just before he died," he told the Mexican. "Somethin' about a 'ransom for General Dodge.' Rickaree was tryin' to tell us something with his last breath, *amigo*. I think Crade Falk can be persuaded to explain what Rickaree meant about the General."

Corinne's night spots were going full blast. Passing a dance hall, they glimpsed a packed floor where booted Irish paddies, cowpunchers and freighters and Easterners were dancing with scantily-gowned, heavily rouged percentage girls, to the blare of a full brass orchestra.

Gunshots smashed out sharply from a

gambling dive at their elbow. The batwings flew open and a bleeding man staggered out, took three steps, and fell in the gutter. An aproned bartender stepped out, a fuming shotgun in his hands. He prodded the dead man with a boot toe and returned to the barroom.

"Corinne," the Rio Kid muttered, "is a tough girl."

They were alongside the shack marked "OVERLAND ENTERPRISES" now. Crade Falk's headquarters.

The Rio Kid pushed ahead of his Mexican *compadre,* loosening his Colt .45 in leather. The door of Crade's place was open for ventilation. Seated at a littered desk was a sallow-faced man wearing black silk sleeve guards and a green eyeshade. He was talking to a middle-aged man and wife, obviously sodbusters who had ridden the U.P. coaches west in search of land.

"Take my word for it, Mr. Snogrum," the clerk was saying with unctuous confidence, as the Rio Kid stepped across the threshold, "Corinne won't always be a wild town. It'll be a metropolis bigger than Ogden or Salt Lake City. Take this block of choice lots here at four hundred dollars each —"

The clerk glanced up from his spread-out plat and scowled at the blue-uniformed interrupter.

"Looking for a bargain in real estate, Captain?"

The Rio Kid shook his head. He knew from Celestino's description that this sunken-cheeked man was not Falk. A plaque on his desk identified him as "Samuel Albright, Clerk, Notary Public."

"I'm lookin' for yore boss," the Rio Kid said. "Got a deal with Falk that we're supposed to settle tonight."

Albright muttered an apology to his potential victims and smirked at the Rio Kid.

"I'm sorry, but Mr. Falk left town earlier this evening and won't be back for two-three days. But I can act in his absence."

But the Rio Kid had already spun on his heel and left the office. Outside the fan-wise splash of light from Falk's office doorway, he shrugged and looked at Celestino.

"Crade Falk flew the coop, Celestino. When the marshal got back tonight with the news about our escape, Falk figgered it might be best to fade out of sight for the time bein'."

They headed over to the Sledge & Spike Hotel to look for the horses Celestino had left ground-hitched in the street after seeing the Rio Kid being ushered out of the hostelry at gun's point. Some thoughtful individual had hitched Saber and the black to the tie-rail for them.

Despite their own needs, the welfare of their mounts came first with the two riders. They located a livery barn, paid the hostler twenty dollars in advance for a single night's grooming and graining for the animals, then hunted up a restaurant which occupied a soddie on a side street.

An unpalatable meal of buffalo steak and chicory coffee, with sourdough biscuits extra, set them back five dollars apiece. They ate greedily, and despite the unsavory cooking, left the soddie feeling immeasurably refreshed.

"Some shut-eye, General?" the Mexican asked hopefully. "We can't go on living on our nerve."

"I've got to report to General Dodge first, Celestino. Accordin' to what Sherman told us, he lives in a private car. I can't shake off the feelin' that Dodge, just because he's chef engineer for the Union Pacific project, is in danger."

They had no difficulty in locating the day coach, shunted on a sidetrack on the outskirts of the railroad yards and which bore a sign:

CHIEF ENGINEER — PRIVATE

Although it was nearly two o'clock in the morning, lights glowed in the coach.

They climbed the iron-railed front platform and rapped on the door. After a short delay, it was opened by a sleepy-eyed cavalry sergeant who, spotting Pryor's insignia of rank, stiffened to attention and brought his arm up in salute.

"Can General Dodge be seen this time of night, Sarge?" asked the Rio Kid.

"He's in conference with Marshal Shelly, sir," said the sergeant. "Unless your business with him is important —"

"It's plumb important, Sergeant."

"All right. Wait inside here till the marshal is finished. I'm Sergeant Arkin, the general's orderly."

The Rio Kid and Celestino found themselves in a forward compartment of the coach which served as the chief engineer's living quarters and office on wheels. Light streamed through a connecting door, and as the two settled themselves on a bench in the shadows, they heard Tom Shelly's high-pitched voice.

"I caught this here captain red-handed in Pickett's hotel room, General Dodge!" the marshal was saying. "I tell yuh, he's a killer! Seein' as how he made his escape outside the town limits, I figger capturin' the walloper is up to the military."

A rumbling bass voice, with overtones of weariness, answered the Corinne lawman. It was the voice of General Grenville Dodge, the man in charge of building the transcontinental railroad.

"Make your report to Colonel Benteen, Marshal," the voice said. "He has charge of the troops, not I. If a killer is on the loose, and if he is, as you say, a member of the armed forces, it is quite possible he will be carried on Colonel Benteen's morning report as absent without leave."

CHAPTER VII

The Golden Dragon

Marshal Tom Shelly appeared in the doorway. His hand gripping the frame of the door, Shelly peered back into General Dodge's office.

"Pardon me for botherin' yuh at this hour of the night, General Dodge," he said, in a servile tone. "But I figgered mebbe this Jesse Pickett was a friend o' the railroad's an' you should be the first to know he was kilt."

"Pickett was a stranger to me," Dodge answered sharply. "Take your report to the Colonel, Shelly."

The Rio Kid's hand was on his gun butt as the marshal turned, his back toward them. But he stepped out of the platform door into the night without seeing them.

When the end-of-track town marshal had left, Celestino whispered excitedly:

"Deed you see the finger ring Shelly was wearing, General?"

The Rio Kid nodded, his eyes grim.

"Yes. I got a close look at it in the lamplight while Shelly was standin' there. A ring in the shape of a golden dragon. Major Ironwall's ring."

A pulse hammered in Celestino's throat as he nodded.

"That golden dragon was taken off a dead man's finger, *no es verdad?* I have a hunch Senor Tomaso Shelly keeled that Army spy."

A shadow fell across the partition doorway. The sergeant, General Dodge's personal orderly, poked his head into the baggage compartment and beckoned to the Rio Kid.

"General Dodge will see yuh, Captain. General Jack Casement is with him." Sergeant Arkin winked. "They're in a bad mood, sir."

The sun-blackened, spade-bearded face of General Grenville M. Dodge, U.S. Army engineer, was drawn with fatigue and the accumulated tautness of responsibilities which would have broken a lesser man months ago. He was seated at a desk covered with blueprints of trestles and tunnels, compound-curve cuts and fills — the multiplicity of paper work and draftsmanship which went into the building of the longest railroad in the world.

Head buried in his hands, elbows on desk, Dodge did not look up immediately when the orderly ushered the hard-bitten young visitor into the office compartment of the coach. The Rio Kid's first welcome came from the scrappy-faced little Irishman who was superintendent of construction for the Union, John Stevens Casement, better known to his paddies as "Gen'l Jack."

"Captain Robert Pryor, sirs, reportin' for special duty by order of the Commander-in-Chief."

Dodge looked up from his desk then, his red-rimmed gray eyes snapping from the blue-clad man to the Rio Kid's Mexican partner.

"I'm General Dodge," he grunted, rising and extending his hand. "General Casement, Captain Pryor."

After the Rio Kid had introduced Celestino, who withdrew to a corner where the sergeant had his post, Pryor turned to the chief engineer and smiled.

"Yuh don't remember me, General. I was a scout under Custer in Sixty-three. I met you at the Battle of Atlanta, when I was an aide to General Tecumseh Sherman. Earlier this week I had a rendezvous with both Sherman and Sheridan out in the Wasatches."

Dodge's tired eyes were inscrutable. Released from the Army on leave following Lee's surrender at Appomattox, Dodge had taken over the Union Pacific project in May of Sixty-six. Since that time he had accomplished engineering miracles, but the heavy toll of his worries had aged the man.

"What is the nature of your special duty, Captain Pryor?" he asked wearily. "Do you have any proof that President Grant sent you to me?"

The Rio Kid briefly explained his discovery of Major Justin Ironwall's murder, and how Marshal Tom Shelly had confiscated his secret orders from Washington. Not until he had finished did a glimmer of interest show in Dodge's eyes.

"You are the Rio Kid?" he said then. "In that case I do indeed recall having seen you during the Georgia campaign, Captain. Pardon my lapse of memory. But troubles have been heaping up on me so much of late that I sometimes even forget Jack Casement's name."

Construction Superintendent Casement eyed the Rio Kid thoughtfully, rubbing his lean Irish jaw.

"Marshal Shelly was just in here, Kid, trying to get Dodge to put a company of troops in the field with orders to shoot you on sight. He claims that our Intelligence man, Major Ironwall, met his death at your hands."

Realizing that the truth was his best defense, the Rio Kid outlined the grim events which had transpired since his arrival in Corinne with Celestino Mireles less than twelve hours before. The imprint of his ordeal was plainly legible on the Rio Kid's face and dust-grimed uniform.

"It appears that Major Ironwall's secret died with him, so I have to work blind on this assignment, sir," the Rio Kid finished his summation. "It's my belief that this marshal, Tom Shelly, is a tool in the hands of a land speculator here in town named Crade Falk. Other than that slight clue, I know nothin' at all about what dangers, present or future, I'm facin'."

It was obvious from the expressions of both Dodge and Casement that they had accepted his story at face value. After a long pause, the chief engineer sighed heavily and started stacking his blueprints. Sergeant Arkin leaped forward to take over the task.

"Trouble comes in bunches," Dodge complained. "It's not enough that I've had to fight fifteen thousand Indians for every inch of right-of-way. It's not enough that the Credit Mobilier is bleeding the stockholders white, trying to bring politics to bear to make me run the Union over as many trestles and through as many tunnels as they can get contractors to build. Now Crade Falk and his crowd are getting ready for a last-ditch stand — with murder no handicap."

Stepping over to the wall of the coach, General Dodge pulled down a large map of northern Utah, showing two red lines entering the Mormon country from west and east.

"I'll show you the set-up we're facing, Rio Kid," he said. "This line coming out of Nevada is Collis P. Huntington's Central Pacific out of California. His Chinese coolies have already laid grades almost to Ogden, paralleling the Union Pacific. As you can see, the U.P. is also running north of Salt Lake. Our right-of-way is building toward the Humboldts in Nevada, right alongside the steel which the Central already has down."

The Rio Kid nodded his understanding.

"Why," he inquired courteously, "can't

the Union and the Central join their trackage to form a single line, instead of duplicatin' each other this way?"

Dodge gave vent to a tirade of barracks room profanity, in which Casement joined him.

"Politics, Captain," Casement cut in harshly. "Greed. Graft. Corruption in high places. When Congress authorized the building of the overland railroad, they passed a law saying we had to buy our steel in America. The factories promptly upped their prices eight hundred per cent above normal. We've had to pay mahogany prices for cottonwood ties."

The Rio Kid smiled sympathetically.

"Accordin' to what General Sherman told me," he said, "Congress may step in and force an end to this duplication of steel, sir. Sherman aims to ask General Grant's support. As our new President, Grant may force the Union and the Central to join their rails somewhere here in Utah."

General Dodge tapped his map with a blunt fingertip.

"And here is where promoters like Crade Falk enter into the troubled picture, Captain," the chief engineer said. "Falk has purchased thousands of acres of land to the south and west of the lake. He's trying everything — I almost said short of murder — to get us to change our plans and route both the Central and the Union south of the lake, to Salt Lake City.

"Brigham Young has preached sermons on the subject in the Mormon Tabernacle. But Young has finally agreed with Charles Crocker of Central and myself that it is not practicable to make Salt Lake our terminus. That's why we're going ahead, laying our steel north of the Lake, through the Promontory Range."

The pattern began to make sense to the Rio Kid now. Its full understanding, he realized, was vital to his own plans.

"As I understand it, then," he said, "Falk stands to go bankrupt if the railroad don't build through land which he aims to sell to settlers and speculators south of Salt Lake?"

"Exactly," snapped Casement. "Worthless salt flats and miles of sand dunes. And to slow down construction, men like Falk have planted labor agitators in my construction gangs, trying to foment discord. I understand they're smuggling opium to Crocker's Orientals, on the Central. It's a vicious business, backed by unscrupulous millionaires both in California and in New York."

★ ★ ★

The Rio Kid fingered his campaign hat thoughtfully.

"I'm beginnin' to see why General Sherman was so worried about the way things are developin' out here," he observed. "And, in view of the odd remarks made by Rickaree just before he died tonight, I have reason to believe, General Dodge, that you may be kidnaped. With your permission, sir, I'd like to become your personal bodyguard from here on. I believe that would have been in line with what Sherman's spy, Major Ironwall, would have told me to do if he'd lived."

Dodge, who had risked his life on unnumbered occasions in the Civil War and as the officer in charge of the Department of the Missouri's Indian campaigns of 1865 and 1866, grinned bleakly.

"So be it, Captain. You and your friend Celestino can attach yourselves to the U.P. boarding train for quarters and rations until this blasted railroad is finished, for all I care."

Captain Pryor saluted, realizing that the interview was terminated.

General Casement gestured toward the far end of the coach.

"If you're going to be bodyguards, you'd

better occupy the spare bunks at the far end of this car, Captain," he suggested. "You both look as if you could stand some rest. Sergeant Arkin, take over."

Minutes later, sprawled at full length in comfortable bunks adjoining Dodge's private sleeping compartment, the Rio Kid waited until Sergeant Arkin had left.

"Celestino," he whispered then, "the first thing ahead of us is to strike at a known target. This marshal, Tom Shelly. He'll know where Falk is hidin' out. I aim to make Shelly talk if I have to ram a hogleg down his throat."

A snore from Celestino was his only answer.

CHAPTER VIII

Good Luck — And Disaster

Sergeant "Red" Arkin took the Rio Kid and Celestino Mireles over to the officers' mess car at the nearby Army camp for a pre-dawn breakfast. The sun's coppery rim was just lifting over the Wasatch Divide when they headed toward main street of Corinne.

The end-of-track town, exhausted after another night's debauch, presented a shabby, drowsy picture in the red light of dawn. Work trains were puffing out of town toward Blue Creek Valley. Flat cars were loaded with rollicking Irish paddies and their soldier escort, their voices lifted in the raucous harmony of the overland railroad's unofficial song:

> Drill, my paddies, drill!
> Drill, you terriers, drill!
> Ho, it's wor-r-rk all day
> Without sugar in yore tay,
> Wor-rkin' on the U. Pay Ra-a-ailway!

General Dodge had supplied the information that the town marshal, Tom Shelly, resided in the Sledge & Spike Hotel when off duty. The trail partners headed toward that canvas-roofed hostelry now.

They found carpenters busy dismantling the poker tables and crating the crystal chandeliers which illuminated the place. The Sledge & Spike, for some reason, was closing down.

No clerk was on duty at the hotel desk, but the Rio Kid consulted the tattered register book and found what he was searching for.

"Shelly's in Room KK, Celestino. That means he's right next door to the room where somebody stabbed Jesse Pickett — Major Ironwall — to death and stole his secret papers."

No one in the barroom paid them any attention as they mounted the rickety staircase and turned left down the foul-smelling hall. A din of snoring came from behind closed doors as they walked down the corridor. Overhead, heat was building up as the Utah sun hit the dirty canvas roof.

Celestino rubbed his palms together in anticipatory glee as the Rio Kid, palming a six-gun gripped the doorknob of Room KK. Immediately to the left was the room where the Army Intelligence man, Ironwall, had been killed yesterday.

The door was locked, but the flimsy catch broke readily before the Rio Kid's battering shoulder. He and Celestino stepped swiftly into the room and wheeled to cover the man sprawled on top of the blanketed cot there, clad in undershirt and cotton drawers.

It was Marshal Tom Shelly, deep in slumber. The lawman's gun-belt hung from a peg on the window frame. His boots, pants and shirt were scattered in disarray on the floor. Dead to the world, Shelly had not stirred as yet.

The Rio Kid appropriated Shelly's six-gun and thrust it under his belt. He drew down the window shade, while Celestino lighted a coal-oil lamp on a packing-box washstand.

Shelly strangled on a snore and sat bolt upright as he felt the cold kiss of a six-gun muzzle prodding his cheek. Major Ironwall's golden dragon finger ring flashed in the lamplight as Shelly sat yawning.

The yawn choked off as the Corinne marshal found himself staring into the black bore of a Colt .45.

"Don't make a sound, Marshal!" the Rio Kid whispered. "We're goin' to have a little palaver before breakfast and yuh'll be a dead man if yuh make a single false move, *sabe?*"

Shelly's eyes lost their sleepy glare and a yellow glint of horror took its place. He shot a glance at the closed door, then at his empty holster hanging from the window frame.

"Yuh — yuh can't git away with this, Pryor!" wheezed the lawman, swinging his sock-clad feet over the edge of the cot. Beneath his underwear, his chest was heaving violently. "The whole town knows yuh're wanted for a killin'!"

The Rio Kid drew up a barrel chair and sat down, holstering his gun. Across the room, Celestino leaned against the taut canvas wall, fingering his own Colt.

"To start the ball rollin', Marshal," the Rio Kid drawled, "where did yuh get that dragon ring yuh're wearin'?"

Shelly's florid countenance bleached bone-white. He started violently, staring down at the glittering ring.

"I — uh — took it off'n Jesse Pickett's finger yesterday. No use buryin' joolry in Boot Hill."

Pryor's lips compressed.

"Yuh mean yuh stabbed Major Ironwall to get that ring."

★ ★ ★

Mention of the name "Ironwall" seemed to shock Tom Shelly like a blow to the solar plexus. Sweat came out in cold drops on his lower lip.

"Yuh — yuh can't prove that kind of talk, Pryor. Yuh're shootin' in the dark."

Pryor swung around to glance at Celestino.

"Hand me yore huntin' knife, pardner. I think the time has come to do a little fancy throat cuttin'."

Shelly leered, convinced that the Rio Kid was bluffing. He laced his hands together over a drawn-up knee as he saw the Mexican hand over a long-bladed Chihuahua *cuchillo,* its edge honed to razor keenness.

Leaning forward, the Rio Kid's left hand shot out, fisting a handful of Shelly's tousled gray hair. Driving Shelly off balance, the Rio Kid leaped up on the bed to pinion down the marshal's arms with his knees.

The terrified lawman felt the point of the knife prick the flesh over his Adam's apple.

"Don't — don't!" he moaned, his eyes rolling in terror. "I — I'll talk. I'll tell yuh — anything — yuh want — to know!"

Pryor eased off the pressure of the knife's point and climbed back to the floor, hauling

Shelly to a sitting posture by the hair.

"That's better," snarled the Rio Kid, pushing his bluff for all it was worth.

Shelly was cracking fast, before the threat of speedy death.

"Wh-what yuh want to know?" he stammered, rubbing the tiny cut on his throat with a palsied hand.

"Where is the man yuh work for — Crade Falk?"

Shelly gulped hard, stared at the knife poised inches from his heart.

"He hid out — somewheres in town," he said shakily, "after I told him yuh'd got out of jail last night. I — I don't know where he's hidin', Pryor, an' that's the gospel truth."

Pryor reamed the point of the *cuchillo* against the flabby skin over Shelly's heart. A whit more pressure, the marshal knew, would drive the blade between his ribs like a hot wire into butter.

"Why was Major Ironwall killed?" the Rio Kid went on inexorably. "Was that Crade Falk's idea?"

Shelly was a trembling wreck now. His one chance to stave off a steel blade lay, he knew, in talking and talking fast.

"Falk found out that Ironwall — Jesse Pickett — wasn't a gambler, like he made out to be," he said. "He found out Ironwall was an Army spy, gettin' the deadwood on what Falk aims to do to force the Central and the Union to run their steel into Salt Lake City."

Celestino Mireles' swarthy face was wreathed in smiles now. They were hitting pay dirt, and with an ease they had not dared hope for.

"Go on, Shelly," urged the Rio Kid. "Don't get ignorant. Tell me everything yuh know about Falk."

Shelly's teeth were clattering with fear now. A small spot of crimson was spreading on his underwear, where the point of Pryor's knife had slit the flesh.

"Falk aims to kidnap the kingpins of the railroad," he blurted. "Gen'l Dodge, Jack Casement, mebbe the U.P. cashier, Durant hisself. He aims to kidnap the Central's kingpins, too — Crocker and mebbe Huntington. Mebbe even Gov'ner Leland Stanford of Californy."

Thoughts were rolling under Bob Pryor's scalp now. The enormity of Falk's plot astounded him. The very existence of the transcontinental railroad was in jeopardy.

"Keep talkin', Shelly," he snapped. "Yuh ain't out of the woods yet by a heck of a long sight."

Shelly moaned despondently.

"That — that's about all I know," he panted frantically. "Figgers if he kidnaps the men back of the railroad buildin', he can force 'em into issuin' orders to run the line south of the Lake. So Falk can clean up a fortune sellin' land along the right-of-way."

The Rio Kid withdrew the pressure of the *cuchillo* blade from the vicinity of the traitorous marshal's wildly throbbing heart.

"Gettin' back to Major Ironwall's killin'," he said. "Who done that?"

"The half-breed who does Falk's dirty work stabbed Ironwall and stole his papers. I — I was takin' a nap in here when I heard somebody snoopin' around Ironwall's room yesterday. That's when I busted in and arrested you."

The Rio Kid shoved the barrel chair to one side and stood up.

"Give me Ironwall's ring, Shelly."

Shelly jerked the golden dragon bauble off his knuckle as if it were a red-hot iron. Pocketing the ring, the Rio Kid handed the bloody-tipped *cuchillo* back to the grinning Celestino.

"I think Shelly has tipped us off to just about what we're up against, Celestino," the Rio Kid said. "I'll take a pasear over to

General Dodge's headquarters and fetch him over to listen to the marshal's story. Meanwhile, you stand guard. If Shelly makes a booger move, cut him to ribbons."

Mireles whetted the knife blade across a sweaty palm and winked at his partner.

"Weeth great pleasure, General. I got the hunch thees marshal keeled Major Ironwall, and not Rickaree, like he say."

Grinning with satisfaction over the outcome of his interview with the cringing marshal, the Rio Kid stepped to the door, glanced up and down the hotel corridor to make sure he was alone, and walked outside.

After Pryor's footsteps died in the direction of the stairway, Celestino and his prisoner eyed each other in silence.

"Young feller," the Corinne marshal said suddenly, licking his lips tentatively, "you look like a smart hombre to me."

Mireles bowed mockingly, hefting his *cuchillo* menacingly.

"Smart enough to cut out your heart weeth one slice, senor."

Shelly made a sickly attempt at a grin. He gestured toward the washstand where the lamp was burning.

"Miracle — er — what's yore name? Son, I've got a bandbox yonder with a thousand dollars in gold. It's —"

Celestino laughed harshly. "Blood money, senor? The *dinero* Falk paid you to keel Major Ironwall yesterday, *quizas?*"

Tom Shelly started to rise, saw the Mexican poise his knife for a lethal thrust, and sat back on the cot.

"Poker winnin's, son. Listen. I'm just a tool. I got no part in this kidnap plot I told yore pardner about. That thousand dollars is all yores, son, if yuh let me drag on my clothes and light a shuck out of Corinne."

Celestino Mireles waggled his head from side to side, his obsidian-black eyes snapping contemptuously.

"Not for a meellion-dollar bribe do I turn you loose, senor. You are going to stretchthos' hangrope, *quizas.*"

A footstep sounded outside the door. The broken lock was jammed and Celestino, anticipating the Rio Kid's return with General Dodge, sidled toward the door to open it, keeping his eye trained on his prisoner. In Shelly's desperate straits, it was conceivable that the man might try a dive through the window.

Pulling open the door, Celestino got a pinched-off glimpse of the man framed there. He recognized the beaver hat and cinnamon mustache of Crade Falk.

A six-gun was in the speculator's hand,

lifted above his head. Before Celestino could duck back to avoid the chopping blow, Falk's gun muzzle smashed hard across the Mexican's temple.

Blackness swirled in a tight vortex about him, and Celestino was not conscious of collapsing on the hotel floor at Falk's feet.

Falk stepped into the room, shoving Celestino's inert bulk out of the way of the closing door. His gooseberry eyes shifted to Tom Shelly.

"What was goin' on here, Marshal?"

Shelly came to his feet, his knees wobbling under him.

"This Mexican and the Rio Kid woke me out of a sound sleep, Crade," Shelly panted. "They was tryin' to make me tell what I knew about yore plans. But I'd of let 'em cut my throat before I'd of double-crossed you, Boss."

Falk shoved his gun into an armpit holster under the lapel of his fustian Prince Albert. He stared down at the Mexican's insensible face for a long moment.

"Drag on yore clothes, Tom!" Falk ordered brusquely. "The time has come for us to drag wagons out of Corinne, I reckon. And I got a hunch this Rio Kid won't be seein' his Mexican partner this side of Hades."

CHAPTER IX

Blind Trail

When the Rio Kid returned to the Sledge & Spike Hotel twenty minutes later, in company with Grenville M. Dodge, he was amazed to see that carpenters had dismantled the false front of the hotel building while workmen were hauling the unbolted prefabricated sections by mule wagon to the railroad yards.

Even as he stared, Pryor saw the long back-bar mirror come down, its prismed sections ready for stowing in the packing cases which formed the bar counter.

"This happens every time end-of-track pushes ahead, Captain," Dodge said as he laughed at the Rio Kid's astonishment. "I've established headquarters at Promontory, west of here. Which means the construction crews won't be coming back to Corinne to buck the tiger after tonight. So the saloons and honkytonks move west. This time tomorrow night, Corinne will have frog-hopped to Promontory."

All up and down the main street, buildings were coming down. But through the boiling dust and confusion, there was order and precision instead of the apparent chaos. For the Rio Kid was witnessing the death of a city. A week from now Corinne would merely be a way station on the Union Pacific, marked by a litter of tin cans and beer bottles, and an acre of Boot Hill cemetery where unmarked grave mounds marked the resting places of scores of human souls who had played out their strings in this wild community.

Where Crade Falk's land office had stood was now a blank patch of hard-packed earth. Even as he put his glance toward the Red Tent Casino where Celestino had seen Crade give Rickaree his orders last night, the vast spread of circus canvas billowed to the ground. Workmen swarmed in to ready the canvas for shipment by flat car to the new boom camp at Promontory.

Dodging through the swarms of carpenters, the Rio Kid led General Dodge up a flight of steps which, he realized, would be dismantled within the hour.

As they walked down the hall toward Shelly's room, blue sky and punishing sunlight were over them. The Sledge & Spike had been stripped of its canvas roof.

"We tackled the marshal in the nick of time." The Rio Kid grinned. "In all this confusion, it wouldn't have been safe for me to have escorted Shelly over to yore private car, General."

Dodge shrugged, his face flushed with anticipation. The Rio Kid had outlined Crade Falk's perfidy, as revealed by Shelly's confession, during their walk over from the U.P. yards.

"Yuh may object to the strong-arm tactics I'll have to use to force the marshal to talk to yuh, General Dodge." The Rio Kid grinned again as they halted before door KK. "But — it might be necessary."

"I don't care a hoot," Dodge cut in, "if you blow Shelly's brains out."

The Rio Kid opened the door. The hot sunlight pouring through the roofless opening revealed a disheveled cot, the lamp still burning on the packing box, but no trace of Celestino Mireles or Tom Shelly.

A quick stab of dismay hit the Rio Kid as he jerked his glance back to the painted letters on the door paneling, thinking he had come to the wrong room.

"Nothing to worry about, Captain," the U.P. engineer grunted, seeing Pryor's scowl.

"Your Mexican friend had to move his prisoner out before the workmen dismantled this upper story."

The Rio Kid was about to accept the General's explanation as the only plausible one to account for the absence of Celestino and the marshal, when he caught sight of a smear of still wet blood on the floor near the threshold.

"No — something's happened!" he rasped. "Some plug-ugly in Falk's pay must have seen us headin' here to badger the marshal in his den. I — I don't like the looks of this, General."

At that moment the canvas walls of Room KK collapsed and two workmen whipped the tarp into a tight roll. Another was busy folding up the cot where Major Justin Ironwall had died, in the adjoining room.

"One side, buckos!" snapped a dismantling foreman, coming down the corridor. He had been opening doors and bellowing to the sleeping tenants as he advanced. "This hotel's got to be erected at end-of-track before sundown tonight."

Returning to the stairway, the Rio Kid and General Dodge found that the steps had already been carted off, a ladder replacing them.

★ ★ ★

Back on the river of churned dust which had been the main street, General Dodge laid a paternal hand on the Rio Kid's shoulder.

"I'm sure nothing has happened to your friend, or the marshal," he said reassuringly. "They'll turn up over at my private car sooner or later."

But an hour elapsed and the Rio Kid, pacing the right-of-way alongside Dodge's headquarters, realized that the General's optimism was groundless.

Disaster had overtaken Celestino during his absence. It was incredible that Tom Shelly could have got the upper hand of the Mexican. More likely, accomplices from Crade Falk's outlaw faction had rescued Shelly. In that case, Celestino might be lying dead in some alley, even now.

The rest of the morning was a nightmare to the Rio Kid. Returning to the livery stable, which he found almost entirely dismantled, pending shipment to end-of-track, he saddled Saber and Celestino's black, taking his mounts over to the Army corral beyond the boarding train.

Then he began a systematic search of the alleys which honeycombed the buildings of Corinne which were still standing, peering under the foundations of houses, poking through piles of debris, fearing at any moment that he might uncover Celestino's bloody corpse.

Freight trains were already pulling out of town, moving west, with their flat cars laden with lumber and rolled tentage which, by sundown, would form another lawless Sodom of the desert.

Despair laid its acid taste on the Rio Kid's tongue when, at high noon, Corinne had lost the look of being a town, and instead was a dust-shrouded scene of confusion. Only the Union Pacific shops and the maroon-painted depot remained to mark the site of the town.

His questions to passing citizens regarding Tom Shelly invariably drew the same reply:

"The marshal's likely gone ahead to Promontory with his jail car, stranger. It's been like that ever since Julesburg and Cheyenne. Tom Shelly leads the exodus to the new promised land."

The Rio Kid stumbled back up the street, his eyes staring as he buffeted throngs of painted honkytonk girls, gamblers and their cohorts. All of them were heading for the passenger train which would take Corinne's citizens on to end-of-track.

A feeling of despondency such as he had never known gripped the Rio Kid now. Celestino had vanished as if the earth had swallowed him. He knew better than to believe that Marshal Shelly had left town with his jail car. He doubted if he would ever lay eyes on the doublecrossing marshal again — or on Celestino either.

Bogged down by a growing sense of frustration and loss, the Rio Kid joined General Dodge for the noon meal, their last in Corinne before the engineer transferred his quarters to Promontory.

"It looks hopeless, sir," Pryor reported, picking at his food without appetite. "Celestino is nowhere in Corinne. I'm dead positive of that. I even checked Boot Hill, to see if any new grave had been dug."

Dodge bent a sympathetic stare at his new bodyguard.

"It shows you the breed of devil we are bucking, Captain. Frankly, I doubt if you'll find Shelly at Promontory. I imagine the railroad will have to hire a new marshal."

The Rio Kid made a second thorough tour of the nearly deserted townsite, in a futile search for his Mexican partner, before catching General Dodge's car at three o'clock for the run west to Promontory. His horse and Celestino's followed in the cavalry section of the troop train.

They pulled into the embryo city of Promontory at four o'clock, where Dodge's private car was shunted onto the siding prepared for it.

Yesterday, Promontory had been a blank desert of sage and catclaw and dwarfed mesquite, at the eastern foot of the mountain range which jutted its promontory out into Great Salt Lake. The only trace of the advent of civilization had been the sprawling yellow grade of the Union Pacific, flanked a few miles north by an identical line being built by Central's coolies.

Now, twenty-four brief hours later, another boom camp had taken root, one destined to be the last sinkhole of lawlessness on the empire-building steel trail.

To the Rio Kid's amazement, he saw the Sledge & Spike Hotel occupying a spot on the main street, looking precisely as he had seen it this morning in Corinne. In a matter of hours, skilled laborers had reassembled the hostelry and opened it for business.

The fabulous "Big Tent," the largest saloon to follow the trail of the Iron Horse out from Omaha, was going up and would be ready by nightfall. From the Red Tent

Casino already came the dry clatter of poker chips and the click of the roulette ball.

A duplicate copy of Corinne was fast taking shape, and inside a week Promontory would be a city of several thousand transients. A malevolent spiderweb, luring the army of Irish paddies and the gullible tourists to lose their gold — perhaps their lives — inside its dismal limits.

Tom Shelly's jail car was on a spur track, but it was minus a marshal. A turnkey who guarded the jail daytimes informed the Rio Kid that in all probability Shelly was over at Room KK in the Sledge & Spike, resting up for his night tour of duty.

Pryor paid the hotel a visit, knowing beforehand that it was a futile waste of time. But so great was his anxiety over Celestino's fate that he was snatching at any straw now.

He found a silk-hatted Boston capitalist occupying Room KK.

Leaving the hotel, he saw that Crade Falk's land office had been erected across the street. It was overflowing with homestead hunters and tenderfeet from east of the Mississippi, scanning the plat which Sam Albright, the clerk, had drawn up for the new "City of Promontory."

Albright's persuasive nasal voice droned in the Rio Kid's ears as he elbowed his way into the crowded land office:

"Now's the golden opportunity to get in on the ground floor and buy lots from Overland Enterprises, gentlemen. Ten years from now, Promontory will be Utah's first metropolis, outshining Salt Lake City. Only five hundred dollars for choice frontage on —"

A Hoosier hayshaker shook a fist under Albright's nose.

"You sold me two lots on Railroad Avenue in Corinne last week, you swindler. Today they're nothin' but a rubbish dump. By jasper, Mr. Albright, you give me my money back or —"

The clerk caught sight of the Rio Kid, and welcomed the interruption.

"Mr. Crade ain't back yet, Captain," he called. "Like I told you, if I can help you with your deal —"

The Rio Kid left the land office in disgust. On his heels came a blasting gunshot, followed by a rush of customers from the shack who almost ran down the Rio Kid in their panic.

Looking back, he saw Sam Albright lying across his desk, a bullet hole punched through his green eyeshade, his lifeblood puddling over the plat of Promontory City. The swindled nester stalked out of the building, holstering a six-gun, and crossed the street in the direction of the Big Tent Saloon.

To Crade Falk's clerk had gone the dubious honor of filling the first grave in Promontory's cemetery.

At dusk the Rio Kid visited the cavalry stables to curry Saber and Celestino's black stallion. He was convinced, now, that the gay-hearted Mexican *hidalgo* would never ride the danger trails at his side again.

Returning to General Dodge's car, he found Sergeant Red Arkin engrossed in sorting a bag of official mail that had just arrived from the East. The freckle-faced noncom glanced up at the Rio Kid and nodded.

"General Dodge has an appointment at end-of-track tomorrow, sir," Sergeant Arkin said. "He's meeting Central's chief engineer, Charles Crocker. As the General's bodyguard, you are expected to go along. There'll be a flat car for your horse."

CHAPTER X

Desert Hideout

Gradually, slowly, Celestino Mireles' tortured brain groped slowly out of the black tunnel of insensibility.

Ruddy daylight — he could not be sure whether it was sunset or dawn of the next day, having lost his sense of direction — limned a rectangular window in a stone wall which flanked his body.

Attempting to sit up, the Mexican *hidalgo* made the discovery that he was trussed up like a cocoon, his arms behind his back, his legs roped at knees and ankles. His neckpiece had been stuffed into his mouth as a gag.

The gradual increase of the light revealed that another day was dawning. So he had been knocked out for a considerable period of time as a result of Crade Falk's pistol-whipping. Hunger pangs added to the agony of his bruised skull, cramping his insides.

Celestino closed his eyes and set about marshaling his scattered thoughts. Chagrin bit deep, mortification over what he felt to be a lack of vigilance on his part in the hotel room in Corinne.

Wherever he was now, he knew this wasn't the railroad camp. His primary sensation was one of being in a vacuum. What sounds reached his ears were internal — the tom-tomming of his heart, the humming sensation in his brain as consciousness slowly was restored.

When he opened his eyes again, the sun's full punishing heat was pouring in through the opening in the stone wall.

He was in a cabin. Rusty tin cans, a rat-chewed lamb's skin, the remains of a canvas chair littered the bedrock floor. The room, about ten feet square, was roofed with mesquite faggots in the *aguaista* fashion which took Celestino back to his native Mexico. It was a popular roofing material for the *jacal* huts of the peon classes.

Rearing himself to a sitting position and jiggling his body around to rest his shoulder blades against the adobe-mortared stone wall, Celestino sized up the other angles of the room. Directly opposite him, on the south wall of the cabin — the angle of the morning sun rays oriented him — was a hewn-slab door which, in lieu of hinges, swung on a pivot made from a Conestoga wagon axle, by way of sockets in the lintel slab and the bedrock threshold. The door was closed, but apparently unlocked.

To the right of the door was a rickety table. A stub of candle was in a cobweb-festooned beer bottle, along with a moldy deck of playing cards.

Crade Falk had secreted him, apparently, in a prospector's shack. A miner's shovel and rust-riddled gold pan, hanging from wall pegs over the table indicated that the builder, or at least the tenant, of this abandoned hovel, had been a mining man.

It was somewhere on the desert, Celestino judged, from the scent of sage in his nostrils, and by the steady increase in temperature. But how far it was from the Sledge & Spike Hotel, or by what means Falk had transported him to this spot, Celestino Mireles could not guess.

By dint of hard effort he managed to inch his back up the wall until he was in a standing position. The only means of locomotion possible was a hopping motion, and he started jiggling his way over to the window in the east wall. A similar aperture was in the west wall of the shack.

Peering out into the glare of the morning sun, his eyes squinted almost shut against the dazzle of the sun on water, it took Celestino several minutes to realize that he actually was looking at a body of water, and not a mirage. A hundred feet down a steep, rubble-carpeted slope, the hill jutted into an emerald lake, white-crusted at the shoreline, which extended for miles to the east before meeting the purple line of the far shore.

"Great Salt Lake!" the thought flashed through Celestino's head. "This cabin must be located on Promontory Point!"

Recalling the shape of Utah's vast inland sea, its blue-green waters six times more briny than the ocean, as seen on the big wall map General Dodge had shown to the Rio Kid, Celestino had a mental picture of the rocky peninsula. It thrust its five-mile-wide barrier into Great Salt Lake's northern extremity. The Promontory was approximately twenty-five miles in length and gave its name to the range of mountains which formed the final barrier to the Union Pacific construction crews.

The grinding sound of steel-shod hoofs on rubble, approaching the shack from the north — in which direction Celestino knew the railroad would be — caused the Mexican prisoner to stiffen in his bonds. Muffled voices reached his ears as two riders dismounted in front of the cabin with a creak of saddle leather.

The slab door swung open on its pivoting axle and Crade Falk ducked under the sandstone lintel. He was followed by the Marshal of Corinne, Tom Shelly.

Both men stood staring at their prisoner, fanning their faces with their hats. Their eyes showed the strain of a gruelling ride and lack of sleep.

"I told yuh this Mexican wouldn't die before we came back, Tom!" Crade Falk drawled. Shrugging out of his fustian coat, he tossed it on the dusty deal table. "Young feller, I hope yuh savvy enough English to answer some questions. That's the one and only reason yuh didn't die in Shelly's room at the hotel in Corinne day before yesterday."

Day before yesterday! As Celestino sagged to his knees, unable to support his weight any longer in a standing position, he realized why he felt so wilted and impotent. He was starving!

Striding across the room, Marshal Tom Shelly jerked the gag out of Celestino's bleeding lips. Reaching to his hip pocket, the lawman took out a knife — Celestino's own Chihuahuan *cuchillo*.

"Things are a little different, eh, my peon friend?" jeered Shelly. "Now it's yore throat that'll get daylight through it if yuh don't talk!"

Celestino, sagging back against the wall, found it difficult to command any vitality with which to put up a defiant front. Death was inevitable at the hands of his captors. Crade Falk's hideout here on the desolate shore of Promontory Point undoubtedly was well hidden, so hope of rescue was out of the question.

"Go ahead, senor, an' cut out my heart eef you weesh," Celestino said feebly. "I weel tell you *nada*."

Crade Falk, lighting a Cuban perfecto, brushed Shelly aside and squatted down before his helpless prisoner. Reaming the glowing end of the cigar against the moist flesh of Celestino's left cheek, he waited until the Mexican winced with agony from the blistered skin.

"We brought yuh out here on hossback, feller," he said, "with the idea of findin' out what this Rio Kid jasper is doin' in Utah, and why the President of the United States is puttin' men like Major Ironwall — blunderin' fool that he was! — on my trail."

Celestino, in his debilitated condition,

could only find the strength to return Crade Falk's steely glare without flinching.

"Let me carve off his ears, Crade!" snarled Tom Shelly, with a sadistic laugh. "Or set fire to his pant legs. I know a few Injun tricks that'll make him loosen his tongue. If it don't I'll cut his tongue out with his own knife."

The land speculator, his face only a trifle less cruel of mouth and eye than that of the bestial marshal at his side, jabbed his burning cigar at Celestino's eyes, forcing the Mexican to writhe frantically in his bonds.

"I make no — *habla*," Celestino gasped desperately. "Torture me, you gringo dog. I weel say nossings!"

Crade turned to Shelly and nodded. The marshal reached for Celestino's right ear, touched the razor-whetted knife to its lobe.

At that instant, the sound of a galloping horse pounding up the rocky slope outside the cabin caused Falk and Shelly to jump to their feet, jerking six-guns from holsters, their torture plans for Celestino momentarily forgotten.

"It's Red Arkin!" Falk grunted, cheeks ballooning with relief as a rider leaped from stirrups in front of the open door. "I thought for a second mebbe —"

Celestino Mireles, on the dizzy edge of oblivion, pulled his eyelids open as he recognized the flushed rider who staggered up to the doorway. It was General Dodge's personal orderly, Sergeant Arkin. And it was obvious from the grins on the faces of his captors that Arkin was a confederate of the evil duo.

"General Dodge is meeting Crocker of the Central over on the summit this afternoon, Crade!" the Army NCO panted. "I managed to borrow a nag and get over from end-of-track. Lucky I knew where your hideout was located, after you skipped out of Corinne day before yesterday."

A slow grin dawned on Crade Falk's drooping mouth. Speaking around his rich-smelling perfecto, the land promoter purred softly:

"A chance to nab the chief engineers of both railroads in one grab. Shelly, we're hittin' the saddle. This is a million-dollar deal we're pullin' today."

Sergeant Arkin's eyes flashed malevolently. He thrust his hand out to Falk, rubbing his thumb and fingertips together.

"How about my pay-off before you get to counting your millions, Crade? I took a risk bringing this tip to you."

Falk, his mind far away, stared at the blue-clad sergeant a moment, then scowled in annoyance.

"I got no cash on me, Red. See my clerk, Sam Albright. He paid yuh off when yuh let us know that Jesse Pickett was an Army Intelligence officer sniffin' our trail, didn't he? Yuh'll find Albright in Promontory. Tell him I said to give you five hundred in gold."

Sergeant Arkin showed a battery of tobacco-stained teeth in a leering grin.

"Uh-uh. Albright's in Promontory, all right. In Boot Hill."

The cigar dropped from Falk's mouth at this shocking news.

"The blazes you say! What happened to old Sam?"

Arkin shrugged. "One of the hillbillies you gypped shot him between the eyes yesterday evening. They buried him this morning as Dodge's train was pulling out of Promontory."

Falk shrugged off the news of his employee's death without visible signs of remorse.

"Well, Sergeant, yuh'll have to trust me for yore rake-off. Yuh'd better get back to end-of-track."

Arkin hesitated, shot a startled glance into the shack at Celestino. Then, recognizing the Mexican as the Rio Kid's missing partner, he eyed Falk and Shelly in turn.

"What are you going to do with the Mexican?"

Falk, donning his coat, bent a long stare at Celestino.

"Reckon we don't need him, Shelly. Pitch him in that poisoned well outside for the time bein'. If he don't drown, the arsenic will fix him."

Celestino, too weak to offer resistance, groaned as the burly marshal picked him up and carried him outdoors. A few yards from the rock cabin, in the direction of a prospect hole burrowed in the side of the slope, was the circular stone combing of a well.

"If I'd had my druthers, I'd have carved yuh up like a Christmas turkey, bucko!" Tom Shelly grunted, halting at the circular rim of the open-top well. "So's yuh won't feel too lonesome, this here's where the Rio Kid'll be put in pickle, 'fore long."

Celestino felt himself plummeting through space, to land with a foamy splash in brackish water ten feet below the ground level. His trussed legs hit bottom, and he was standing in armpit-deep depth.

The rock wall of the well, dug by the prospector who had built the shack, was crusted with a greenish smear which told the trapped Mexican that arsenic deposits were in this water. The poison-infused water would kill him if thirst drove him to take a drink.

Peering up at the white disk of the Utah sky, he saw Tom Shelly's head and shoulders overhead. Then the diabolical marshal vanished from sight.

CHAPTER XI

Rails West

Bob Pryor was not prepared for the full dramatic impact of the scene which met him at end-of-track. For leaving the private car which had brought him and General Dodge from Promontory at daybreak, he found himself witnessing the actual westward march of the rails.

The full import of the bustling industry here in the Promontory Range foothills was beyond description. The legion of Irish paddies under the command of Jack Casement were engaged in a race against time and distance which had no precedent in American annals.

Off and away into the Promontory uplands stretched the new gravel roadbed which the grading crews had built the week before, following survey stakes driven by Dodge's engineers. Private contractors had already made the cuts and fills, thrown up the wooden trestles, bridged canyons and drilled tunnels through mountains.

Now, before the Rio Kid's eyes, he was treated to the actual laying of the steel on which transcontinental trains would haul passengers and mail and freight from coast to coast.

Walking toward the west with General Dodge at his side, the Rio Kid passed waiting flat cars stacked with iron rails from Pennsylvania mills, to the ultimate end of the line. Here a light car, drawn by a single white horse, galloped to the front with its load of rails.

Two burly paddies seized a rail and, helped by other Irish giants working in pairs, lifted the rail off the car. They trotted up the line of cross ties which the tie-laying gangs had set and leveled in the ballasted grade.

Up ahead through the dust, Jack Casement shouted a command, and the rail was lowered. Another crew, working from the opposite side of the car, placed a parallel rail into position on the ties. Less than thirty seconds to the rail, four rails to the minute, and the steel was ready for the spikers.

Sledges hammered rhythmically in triple time. Ten spikes to the rail. The process was repeated, its speed dazzling the Rio Kid's comprehension.

No sooner had the Irish anvil chorus disposed of the carload of steel than the car was tipped over on its side to permit the next car to progress to end-of-track. A teamster, driving a mule at the end of a sixty-foot tow-rope, waited until the empty car was set back on the rails, then towed it back to the supply train for a fresh load.

"That's the way it goes, Captain," General Dodge grinned, noting the Rio Kid's rapt attention to the thrilling spectacle. "Four hundred rails to the mile, sometimes seven miles to the day. Eighteen hundred miles to San Francisco and salt water. You can see how this business gets in a man's blood. Makes him forget the danger of Indian attack, the rottenness of the politicians and money-lenders who are backing — or impeding — the whole shebang."

The Rio Kid could only shake his head in bewilderment. He knew that back of this end-of-track drama were a thousand problems. Like policing wild towns like Corinne; getting supplies on time from the East, where Jack Casement's brother had charge of this angle of the stupendous project.

Timber cutters, a veritable army of them, had scoured the reaches of plain and desert for wood to supply the cross ties.

Grading the right-of-way, crossing mountains by hitherto undiscovered passes, bucking the snows of blizzard-bound winters and the suns of desert summers — all these things, and a million other facets as well, went into the building of the Union Pacific.

And at its head, as chief engineer, was the guiding genius of the man at his elbow, Grenville M. Dodge, still on the sunny side of forty.

"On the other side of this range," Dodge said, waving a hand toward the heat-shimmering uplands before them, "Huntington's Chinese are shoving steel toward us. You'll get to meet Central Pacific's chief later this afternoon."

Two cavalry privates came forward, leading a powerful bay which was Dodge's personal mount, and the Rio Kid's dun, Saber.

"You got a fine saddler here, Captain," said an admiring onlooker. "The 'breed that never dies.' You can tell from that stripe down his back."

The Rio Kid, swinging into stirrups, patted Saber's mane affectionately.

"He was foaled with Civil War cannon smoke in his nostrils," Pryor said. "Saber's like a brother to me. Wouldn't say he has such a good disposition though. Woe to anybody who tries to ride him, except me. Or to any hoss that comes near when he's got a mad on."

Riding stirrup to stirrup, General Dodge and his bodyguard rode out of the dust and racketing confusion, flanking the right-of-way until they were ahead of the spikers and rail-layers.

The Rio Kid twisted around in saddle as they reined up onto the unrailed cross ties and pushed west toward their rendezvous with Charles Crocker, the Central's chief engineer.

"It gives you a lot to think about when you realize that one of Julius Caesar's Roman chariots was responsible for the gauge of this railroad you're building, General," Pryor commented idly.

Dodge stared at his bodyguard curiously. "What?" he asked.

"Why two thousand years ago, the wheels of Roman chariots were spaced four feet, eight and one-half inches apart," the Rio Kid said. "Later, when the Britons made their first wagon, they adopted that gauge to fit the ruts of Roman highways. American Conestogas and Studebakers and Concords were built to the same gauge, so it followed that when stagecoaches were mounted on rails to be drawn by the first locomotive in the seventeen hundreds, railroads had their rails four feet, eight and one-half inches from center to center. In the South, they use a five-foot gauge, which is a lot more practical. When the War broke out, President Lincoln tried to make the standard American gauge five feet, but a Northern Congress clung to the old Roman chariot gauge."

He broke off, grinning embarrassedly. "I hope, General," he apologized, "I haven't been borin' yuh with my erudition."

Dodge threw back his head and laughed.

"On the contrary," the U.P. chief said, "I thank you for the educational tid-bit. I've built a lot of railroad line in my time, but I never knew the story back of our standard gauge before."

Five miles west of the end-of-track gangs, they passed the tie-laying crews, who gave Dodge a cheer as the two riders galloped past. Soon they were in a deep ravine, the barren slopes of the Promontory summit looming on both sides of them. They rode in moody silence, Dodge's mind filled with his manifold technical problems, the Rio Kid's thoughts reverting to Celestino and his mysterious fate.

By mid-afternoon they had reached a signpost marking the summit of the Promontory Range. A lone horseman rode out of the chaparral and waved to them as they approached.

It was Charles Crocker, the peppery little engineer who had charge of the Central Pacific's army of Chinese laborers. Only a mile distant, in another canyon, the Central's crews were laying steel through the Promontory divide.

"Captain Robert Pryor — meet Charlie Crocker," Dodge said, leaning from stirrups to shake the hand of his rival. "Pryor's my bodyguard, Crocker."

Amenities dispensed with, Dodge said mischievously:

"The vice-president of the Union, T. C. Durant, is wagering ten thousand dollars that Casement's Irish paddies can lay ten mile of rail in a day. You think your yellow men can match that, Charlie?"

Crocker spat a gobbet of tobacco juice into the dust and laughed uproariously.

"We've taken Durant's bet, General. My Celestials can lay two rails to your Emerald Isle boys' one."

Dodge's bantering mood passed, as he remembered his reasons for arranging this rendezvous.

"Charlie, let's get over into the shade yonder," he said. "I want to sound you out on whether Huntington and Mark Hopkins and Governor Stanford are going to insist on this crazy idea of building the Central all the way into Ogden — when the U.P. is already running trains west of Ogden."

Crocker did not reply until the three men had dismounted, picketed their horses on the shady side of the canyon, and had withdrawn to a cool spot to hunker down for their discussion.

"Central will build a parallel track all the way to Omaha, so far as the big-money boys in California are concerned, General," Crocker said gravely. "You and I, as engineers, see the folly of such a procedure. But it is out of our hands."

Dodge's finger traced a pattern in the dust.

"It is up to you and me to talk some sense into the bigwigs' empty noggins, Charlie. Personally, I'll lay you a bet that President Grant will force our two railroads to make a common junction somewhere around our Promontory station. Politics should have no place —"

Dodge's words were blotted out by the

roar of a gunshot from the depths of the chaparral. Even as the Rio Kid's hand stabbed to gun-butt, his eyes questing for a telltale smudge of gun-smoke, a harsh voice ripped through the oppressive silence:

"Get yore arms up, the three of yuh! Yuh're under a drop. The first man to dig for steel gets a slug in the brisket."

Crocker and Dodge, neither of them armed, got to their feet and raised their arms jerkily. The Rio Kid, hand frozen on his Colt stock, felt a gun muzzle prod his spine.

Rising, the Rio Kid turned around, to find himself staring into the red-shot eyes of Marshal Tom Shelly. At the same instant a low cry from General Dodge made him jerk his head around to the front.

Stalking out of the chaparral came the blackcoated figure of the missing speculator, Crade Falk. Twin six-guns jutted from Falk's hands as he advanced toward the two engineers.

CHAPTER XII

Ransom Demand

Night had fallen over the rocky backbone of Promontory Point when Falk and Shelly hazed their three distinguished prisoners up to the prospector's shack overlooking an arm of Salt Lake. A cool, salt-laden breeze off the blue platter of water fanned the temples of Dodge and Crocker and the Rio Kid when, helpless before the menacing guns of their kidnapers, they climbed out of stirrups.

Ushering the prisoners into the one-roomed shack, Crade Falk lighted the beer-bottle candle on the table. Confronting the trio of kidnap victims over leveled .45s, the land promoter bit out an order to the grinning marshal.

"Hog-tie these gentlemen, Tom. Then we'll talk business."

Knowing that any show of resistance would bring instant death, the saddle-gaunted trio stood motionless while Shelly lashed their arms behind their backs with rope he had brought along for the purpose.

He followed that up by trussing their legs.

When the three prisoners were seated on the rocky floor with their backs to the wall, Crade sat down on the rickety table beside the flickering candle and thrust his Colts into their concealed holsters under his fustian steelpen coat.

"What's the meaning of this outrage, Falk?" demanded General Dodge. "Why have you brought us here?"

Not once during the afternoon had their captors mentioned the motives behind the kidnaping. But the Rio Kid, recalling what the half-breed Rickaree had said about a "ransom for General Dodge" a moment before he died with Celestino's bullet in his lung, believed he knew what Falk was going to say.

"You two gentlemen," Falk said, indicating Dodge and Crocker, "dictate the route which your railroads will take. An official order from you, General Dodge, would divert the Union Pacific into Salt Lake City. A similar order from you, Mr. Crocker, would swing the Central Pacific around the south shore of Salt Lake, to a common terminus."

Falk grinned malevolently in the candleshine, giving his words a moment to soak in.

"I think I get it," Dodge snarled angrily. "You stand to clean up a fortune with your crooked investment company, Falk, if the railroad goes south of Salt Lake instead of north, the only feasible route from a practical engineering standpoint."

Falk bowed, plucking a cigar from his coat pocket and biting off the tip.

"Exactly, General. Yuh are bein' held for ransom. Yore personal safety can be bought with a scratch of the pen. An order which will send the U.P. through territory I own."

The Rio Kid watched Dodge carefully, saw the engineer's chest rising and falling under his rope bonds.

"And if I refuse?"

Falk shrugged. "Yuh'll be dead before another sunset, General. Along with yore bodyguard, the Rio Kid, and Crocker here. Yuh'll realize I'm desperate if I'm willin' to take such measures. I can't let yore pigheadedness stand between me and my associates in the investment business makin' our fortunes."

Dodge gave vent to a blistering oath.

"Go ahead and shoot, you crooked swindler! I'll sign no such order."

Charles Crocker, seated at the Rio Kid's

left, drew in a deep breath and said vehemently:

"That goes for me too, Falk. Central Pacific will never survey a line south of the Lake. You've got the same answer I gave Brigham Young and his influential Mormons. It isn't practical to make Salt Lake City the terminal. For reasons too abstruse for your demented intelligence to grasp."

Crade Falk slid off the table, bent over to light his cigar from the guttering candle, and then turned to face his captives.

"Yuh'll have overnight to change yore minds, gentlemen. My friend Shelly and I are livin' with a Basque sheepherder up in the hills, since the water supply at this place is poison. However, we will be back at sunup for yore answer."

Marshal Shelly, following Falk to the door, scratched his head dubiously.

"Reckon I ought to stay on guard tonight, Boss?"

Falk flicked ash from his cigar.

"If yuh tied those knots securely, they can't get loose. Yuh haven't eaten since sunrise, Shelly. Suit yoreself."

Falk stepped out into the gathering dusk. After a moment's delay, during which

Shelly checked the knots which bound his three prisoners, the doublecrossing marshal finally left the shack.

Before long Falk reined his horse over to the open window and called down to the prisoners:

"Think it over, Dodge and Crocker. Yore lives in exchange for a simple order for a new survey."

Dodge cranked his head around to stare at Falk.

"You can shoot us now and get it over with, Falk. Our decision will be the same tomorrow as it is now. You and Shelly can go to blazes!"

Falk's taunting laugh was their only answer. There came a rataplan of departing hoofbeats which soon died in the air.

"Looks like our fish is fried, General," Charles Crocker cawed huskily. "Even if we danced to Falk's tune, the devil would kill us anyway, once he got our resurvey orders in his hands."

Dodge settled his spine into a more comfortable position against the rock wall of their prison.

"Obviously," the U.P. engineer grunted. "This is our last sleep this side of eternity, friends. We might as well make the most of it."

After a long pause, the Rio Kid spoke up half-humorously:

"President Grant sent me out here from Santa Fe to be yore bodyguard, General. I reckon I'll start doin' somethin' about guarding yore body pronto."

The Rio Kid hitched his spurred boots under him and, with a mighty effort, wriggled his body upright. Then, precisely as Celestino Mireles had done in this same room some fifteen hours before, Pryor started jiggling his way inch by inch across the stone floor toward the table.

Dodge and Crocker stared with mounting curiosity as they saw the Rio Kid make his slow and painful way alongside the table. Stooping forward, bracing himself against the deal boards to maintain his balance, Pryor nudged the beer-bottle candlestick over to the table edge.

"By jingoes, General, I think you've got a real bodyguard, at that!" Crocker cried out, as a glimmering of the Rio Kid's purpose penetrated his mind, forcing out the terror which was growing there. "Good luck to you, my boy!"

Turning his back to the table, the Rio Kid shoved the ropes which bound his wrists against the trembling candle flame. Guided by verbal directions from the two engineers who watched in fascinated awe, the Rio Kid maneuvered the hempen cords into the hot core of the candle flame.

"Just hope a gust of wind doesn't put this candle out before my ropes are burned through, *amigos*," the Rio Kid said, wincing as the flame blistered the flesh of his palms.

Dodge and Crocker averted their eyes, unable to watch the Rio Kid endure the torture which went with his getaway scheme.

Minutes dragged by, agonizing in their slowness, but one by one the flame ate through the sisal strands.

Sundown glow burned out over Promontory Point. The breeze freshened, guttering the candle flame. The odor of scorching flesh blended with the cloying scent of charring rope.

Finally, after an eternity, the Rio Kid flexed the powerful muscles of his wrists, felt his bonds loosen.

Another five minutes at the flaming candlewick, and the bonds finally snapped asunder.

"Praise be!" panted General Dodge devoutly, as he saw Bob Pryor, shuddering from the pain of his burned hands, clawing at the ropes which bound his legs. "We're free!"

In no more than five minutes the three men walked out into the blue night. Saber whinnied and trotted forward. Down the slope, the horses the two engineers had ridden were grazing in a patch of grass caused by a seep.

"General," the Rio Kid said after the two men had finished shaking his hands in gratitude too deep for words to express, "I suggest that you and Mr. Crocker return to headquarters at Promontory pronto. Yuh'll probably run into soldiers scoutin' for yuh."

Dodge, climbing into saddle, peered down at his bodyguard.

"You'll come with us, of course?"

The Rio Kid shook his head.

"Falk and the marshal will be back at sunrise. I aim to be here to welcome them on the start of their road to the gallows."

Crocker, tightening his saddle girth, bent a shocked look in the Rio Kid's direction.

"Without guns? You'd be trapped like a rat, son."

The Rio Kid grinned and tapped the walnut stock of his Springfield .45-70, which still reposed in Saber's saddleboot.

"I'll have the advantage of surprise to offset my two-to-one odds, Mr. Crocker," he said. "I won't try to look up this Basque sheepherder where they are campin' tonight. I'll just wait for them to re—"

An unearthly, megaphoning cry met the Rio Kid's ears in that moment, a sepulchral sound which seemed to issue, ghostlike, from the very ground on which they were standing.

"General! *Madre de Dios,* help me!"

Wheeling, his heart slamming his ribs, the Rio Kid headed in the direction of the feeble voice. Instinct led him to the black maw of the prospector's arsenic-tinctured well, uphill from the stone shack.

"Eet ees me, Celestino!"

The next moment, his heart overflowing with thanksgiving for this miracle, the Rio Kid was peering down into the murky depths of the well.

Starlight winked on the disk of water ten feet below, and he saw the tortured face of his lost partner peering directly up at him.

"Hold on, *amigo!*" he shouted. "I'll rig my lariat and crawl down after yuh in two ticks!"

Celestino, enervated beyond his powers of endurance by his day-long battle against unconsciousness and drowning in the poisoned waters, was insensible when the Rio Kid, getting a rope around the Mexican's body, had General Dodge haul them to the ground level, with Saber pulling on the 'lass-rope.

The Rio Kid, feeling his partner's feeble pulse, glanced up at the two engineers and shook his head.

"I'll have to forego the pleasure of capturin' Falk and the marshal," he said grimly. "Celestino may be dyin'. I've got to get him to the Army hospital car in Promontory at once."

CHAPTER XIII

Telegram from Grant

Red Arkin, the cavalry sergeant on detached duty with General Granville Dodge in the capacity of the engineer's clerk and personal orderly, sat at his desk in the headquarters car after breakfast the following day, back in Promontory.

There was a stack of mail to sort into piles for the attention of Jack Casement and the chief engineer. But the traitorous noncom was in no hurry. General Dodge would never return from his jaunt into the Promontories to read his letters and telegrams. Dodge was probably dead by now.

It had been more than a year ago that Arkin's association with Crade Falk had begun. That had been when U.P. headquarters were established at Evanston, near the Wyoming line, while the Irish construction gangs fought blizzards in the Wasatch Range in their mad race to beat the Central Pacific into Ogden.

The land speculator, noting Arkin's propensity for hard liquor and gambling during his off-duty hours, had appraised the sergeant for a man who had his price. It was essential to the success of Crade Falk's business, Overland Enterprises, that he have secret advance knowledge of where Dodge planned to build the westering railroad.

Sergeant Arkin, as the chief engineer's confidential secretary, was a logical source of information into the secrets of the U.P. Over a span of months, the wily promoter had cultivated Arkin's friendship and confidence.

Finally, when Crade Falk had become positive he had Arkin on the hook, he made his first proposition — and Arkin had risen to the bait. From then on, Falk had been able to buy land flanking the U.P. right-of-way weeks in advance of his competitors. And, selling that land to gullible speculators who flocked to end-of-track with every incoming train from Omaha, Falk had banked nearly a quarter of a million dollars' illegal profit in the months that had followed his liaison with the treacherous orderly.

Now Arkin, his routine work finished, unbuttoned the blouse pocket of his uniform and took a quick glance at his own bank book. The total of his balance was gratifying — nearly ten thousand dollars which Crade Falk had paid him was deposited to Arkin's credit at his hometown bank in Missouri.

His highest "fee" — a thousand dollars in gold — had been paid him only a week ago for tipping off Falk and his henchman, Tom Shelly, that an Army Intelligence officer was on the trail of Overland Enterprises. As a result of his passing on that top-secret information from General Dodge's office, Major Justin Ironwall had died with six inches of cold steel in his heart, a killing which would never be traced to Marshal Shelly.

Arkin started violently when the door opened and Jack Casement, the construction superintendent, came in for his mail.

"I'm worried about Dodge, Sergeant!" Casement snapped. "This car should have remained at end-of-track yesterday instead of returning here. The General didn't intend to live over in Crockett's C.P. camp."

The noncom gave him his engaging smile.

"Sir, General Dodge told me he might be gone a week. He said he'd send a courier for his car when he's finished with Crocker."

Jack Casement muttered to himself and, picking up his mail, hurried out of the car to catch the next work train to end-of-track.

An hour later, when Sergeant Arkin was engrossed in roseate daydreaming over the amount of Judas bounty Crade Falk would pay him for sending General Dodge and the Rio Kid into his trap, the door suddenly opened and a ghost entered the office compartment.

It was the ghost of General Granville Dodge, haggard and gaunt. Dodge, who should be lying dead in Falk's hideout cabin on Promontory Point!

"Attention, Sergeant!" Dodge snapped angrily. "You're still in the Army, you know. I should take your stripes away from you for bringing my car back to Promontory."

Arkin's head spun as he staggered to his feet and saluted. Something was wrong, terribly wrong. Had Falk and Shelly muffed their golden opportunity to kidnap Dodge and Crocker yesterday?

"At ease — at ease," Dodge groaned, sinking into his chair and eyeing his stack of mail with a shudder. "I've been through Hades since I last saw you, Sergeant."

Briefly, while every word he spoke was

like a coffin nail being driven into Arkin's eardrums, Dodge outlined the gist of his adventures at the hands of Falk and Shelly.

"The Rio Kid's over at the hospital car now, with the young Mexican we found in the well," Dodge finished up. "Celestino's in bad shape, but he'll live. He had quite an ordeal of it . . . And now, clear out, Sergeant. This correspondence won't give me a chance to catch up on my sleep."

Arkin saluted and lurched to the back end of the car, horror pulling at his raw nerves.

"The Rio Kid's Mexican partner is here — and alive!" Arkin's brain raced in an irrational maelstrom. "When he comes to, he'll let the Rio Kid know that I'm Falk's spy in headquarters!"

Something snapped in the sergeant's brain then. He must run — desert the Army — get away from Dodge and the swift retribution which the General would mete out when his sergeant's treachery became known.

Scrambling off the rear platform of the coach, Arkin fled across the tracks. An outgoing freight train, hauling timber and barrels of spikes for Casement's Irishmen at end-of-track, was pulling out of the yards. Leaping for a grab-rail on the fly, Arkin pulled himself onto a flat car and flung himself between two crates of iron fish-plates.

He must rejoin his partners in crime out on Promontory Point. That much was clear in Arkin's deranged mind — and that was all. . . .

Back in his private car, General Dodge picked up a telegram from the White House in Washington D.C. marked *"Urgent."* Scanning the telegrapher's scrawl on the flimsy sheet, a broad grin broke the harsh lines of fatigue on the engineer's face.

Rising, Dodge went to the door and bellowed into Sergeant Arkin's compartment:

"I want you to run over to the hospital car with a message to Captain Pryor, Sergeant Arkin!"

Silence. Flushing angrily at his orderly's incompetence, Dodge clapped his campaign hat on his head and, leaving his car, walked down the length of the U.P. boarding train to the white-painted hospital car at its far end. The car was marked by a red cross, and the Army Medical Department's caduceus insigne.

Entering the car, Dodge brushed past a harassed medical corpsman and approached a bed where Celestino Mireles was being fed his first meal in three days.

Seated at his bedside was the Rio Kid, his burned hands and wrists swathed in bandages.

"Captain Pryor — don't stand up, man — I just got the news I've been praying for, from the President. My worries are over. Take a look at this telegram."

G. M. Dodge, General U.S.A.,
Chief Engineer, U.P.R.R.
Promontory, Utah

Joint house and senate resolution approved today provides that the common terminus of the Union Pacific Railroad Company and the Central Pacific Railroad Company shall be at or near Ogden. The rails shall meet at Promontory summit and connect and form one continuous line.

My congratulations. I am sorry affairs of state will prevent me from being present at the forthcoming wedding of the rails.

     Ulysses S. Grant, President
     United States of America

Captain Bob Pryor came to his feet and, forgetting military regulations, seized his superior officer's hand and shook it vigorously.

"Congratulations, sir. I know what this means to you. No more bickering with greedy politicos and chiseling contractors —"

"Sherman" — Dodge grinned — "did a fine job on Congress."

The smile faded from the Rio Kid's face then. Glancing at Celestino, who was grinning as he sipped his hot gruel, Pryor followed General Dodge out of the hospital coach.

"Sir," he said gravely, "I have shockin' news for yuh. The first thing Celestino told me after the effects of his brain concussion wore off was that our kidnappin' yesterday was the result of the work of a spy in yore own command. The same spy betrayed Major Ironwall."

Dodge stared at the Rio Kid incredulously.

"A spy? Close to my headquarters? You — you don't mean —"

"Yore orderly, Sergeant Arkin. Celestino saw him meet Falk and Shelly at the prospector's cabin on Promontory Point. Falk has been bribin' Arkin for secret information."

Dodge fisted his powerful hands, his face purpling.

"Why, I'll have that traitor before a firin'

squad before —" The chief engineer broke off, remembering something. "Captain," he said numbly, "I'm afraid Arkin has already skipped for parts unknown. I've already told him Celestino was back...."

The eyes of America and the entire world were turned on Promontory, Utah, during the week which followed.

News of the Congressional edict requiring the Central and Union to join rails here on the Utah desert put an end to years of political maneuvering by contractors who were paid lavishly for each mile of rail which was built. Celebrities from all over America began converging on Ogden, to be on hand for the momentous event which President Grant had so poetically termed the "wedding of the rails."

Telegraph lines flashed the news to an excited nation that Vice President Durant of the Union Pacific had lost a $10,000 wager to the Central Pacific. The C.P.'s picked Chinese crew had laid more than ten miles of rail in twelve hours to establish a new world's record.

The Rio Kid brought Celestino the news, which was the prime topic of the day. The Mexican youth was convalescing under a doctor's care in the hospital car.

Crocker's inspired coolies had moved more than four million pounds of material in less than eleven hours to win the bet from Durant, placing twenty-five thousand eight hundred ties in position. They had strung three thousand five hundred and twenty steel rails weighing six hundred pounds each, and had handled more than seven thousand fishplates, fourteen thousand bolts, and fifty-five thousand spikes.

"What makes the U.P. mad," the Rio Kid chuckled, "is that they can't try to beat that record because there ain't ten miles of open grade left between the rail ends now. Crocker was smart."

Celestino Mireles eyed his rugged partner affectionately.

"*You* should have gone out to see thees amazing contest, General," he said regretfully, "eenstead of staying by my bedside. I am *muy bueno*. Tomorrow, thos' medico say I am well again."

The Rio Kid slapped the Mexican playfully.

"*Amigo,* after givin' yuh up for dead, I don't want to let yuh out of my sight again. Life wouldn't be worth much without you for a pardner, old son."

The following day, May ninth, Celestino emerged from his hospital bed completely recuperated from his grim ordeal. His reunion with his black stallion brought tears to the eyes of the cavalry hostlers who witnessed it. Already, Celestino was a popular figure at the Promontory barracks.

Tomorrow, May tenth, 1869, had been set as the momentous day in American history when the rails would meet. Out from California was a special luxury train carrying Governor Leland Stanford, Mark Hopkins, the financier, and the C.P.'s mainspring, Hollis P. Huntington.

Celebrities were beginning to converge on Promontory. The various deadfalls and honkies sensing that their evil flourish was about gone forever, set the town wide open with whisky flowing like water, and gamblers playing for sky-high stakes.

Already the town was jammed with Irish paddies, their work done. Only a single rail's length separated the Central and the Union on this balmy May evening. News had gone out that the Territory of Nevada had shipped a laurel-wood tie and a silver spike from the renowned Comstock Lode for the historic ceremony. Her sister territory of Arizona had matched it with a spike of iron, silver and gold alloy.

But the actual last spike, which was to be driven with a silver sledge-hammer, had been contributed by California. It was made of pure gold from the Mother Lode scene of the gold rush of Forty-nine. Chosen to drive the "Last Spike," after considerable bickering and jealousy were Governor Stanford of California, representing the Central Pacific, and Vice President Durant of the U.P.

The Rio Kid and Celestino, aware that their duties were not finished as long as Crade Falk and Tom Shelly remained at large, stuck close by the man President Grant had dispatched them to Utah to protect — General Dodge.

As a result of their official duties, and at Dodge's insistence, the Rio Kid and his Mexican partner were given seats of honor at the gala banquet which the chief engineer held in his private car that night, honoring Durant and other prominent Union officials.

CHAPTER XIV

Dynamite Plot

Having a banquet and celebration on tap, the Rio Kid could not be a witness to certain clandestine events which were transpiring out on the desert where the Golden Spike was to be driven on the morrow.

The historic spot was deserted save for a telegraph man who was adjusting instruments which would flash the news of the driving of the Last Spike to the waiting world. Everyone else — Irish paddies, blue-clad troopers, Mormons and buffalo hunters and gamblers and painted ladies, regular Army soldiers from Fort Douglas, cowboys from the plains — this vast multitude of America's cross-section of humanity had gathered in Promontory for an historic all-night jamboree.

Out of the night-blanketed canyon-gashed slopes of the Promontory Point peninsula, three riders advanced on the meeting point of East and West, trailing a pack burro. Crade Falk rode in the lead, his face dour in the gloom, his brain poisoned with a lust for revenge which had disjointed his sanity to a degree.

Behind him came the fugitive Marshal of Corinne, aware that the noose awaited him if he were captured. For Major Ironwall's killer was known now. Bringing up the rear was the Army deserter, Sergeant Red Arkin, towing the pack burro. It was laden with a keg of blasting powder, two cases of dynamite, and a package of detonation caps and fuse wire, which they had filched from an old mining claim in the back hills.

These three had spent the past week in hiding, for after Arkin had joined them at the Basque sheepherder's, Falk knew that General Dodge would send soldiers combing the brakes of Promontory Point in search of them. And Falk's fears were well-founded.

The widely contrasting temperaments of the three confederates were welded by the common bond of their outlawry and villainous personalities. Each had his personal motive for embarking on tonight's diabolical journey.

Falk, as a result of the Rio Kid's escape with the kidnaped engineers, knew that he could never draw his loot from a San Francisco bank without facing arrest and execution. His entire world had crashed about his shoulders. Revenge was his prime reason for existing now.

Marshal Tom Shelly realized his own danger if he were captured, for the part he had played in the kidnaping of Crocker and Dodge, to say nothing of Ironwall's death. And Sergeant Arkin knew only too well the punishment that would be given to any Army deserter, a traitor to the confidence General Dodge had reposed in him.

Nearing the telegrapher's shack, the three renegades saw the railroad tracks approaching from east and west, silver ribbons in the light of a new moon. Only a rail's length separated them. All the ties had been set in the roadbed with the exception of two — the laurelwood timber from Nevada, and the historic "Last Tie," of solid mahogany, into which the "Golden Spike" would be driven by a sledge of solid silver.

They reined into the shelter of a motte of smoketrees fifty yards south of the right-of-way and waited until the telegrapher, his work completed, picked up his lantern and set off in the direction of Promontory. He was eager to join the riotous crowds at the boom camp's fleshpots.

Then, moving swiftly out of the darkness, the trio of conspirators went to work.

"I was a telegraph operator myself before I went into the land-sellin' business," Crade Falk chuckled in the darkness, as he helped the marshal and the Army sergeant unpack the explosives from the burro. "My knowledge of electricity comes in handy tonight, I reckon."

Silently, wasting no speech, the three set to work digging an excavation in the roadbed immediately below the spot where the last two ties of precious wood would be placed on the morrow. They worked with rusty shovels obtained from the mining claim they had looted, the shaft-house of which had been their hideout when General Dodge's Army scouts had searched the badlands for them.

When the hole was finished, Crade Falk set the keg of blasting powder and the two cases of dynamite into the excavation, and, working by moonlight, skillfully fashioned percussion caps to interconnecting copper wires linking the explosive charges. Falk then strung his lead wire through a furrow which Arkin had shoveled across the roadbed. It led to a spot where the Army telegraph man had left two wire-ends protruding from the underground cable which led to the instrument board in a nearby tent.

"This red wire," Falk explained, "is goin' to be attached to the Golden Spike tomorrow. The black one goes to a silver sledge that the bigwigs will use to drive this here spike, and that'll complete the electric circuit."

He pointed to the row of telegraph poles which stretched off into the night, both east and west.

"When the sledge hits this Golden Spike," Falk went on, "it'll send a telegraph signal all over the nation. And it'll also send a shot of juice along this detonator wire of ours."

Arkin and Shelly went to work shoveling gravel and dirt over the explosives and the wire which led over to the main cable. Its connection was buried in the telegrapher's original furrow.

The extra dirt from the excavation, representing the cubic content of the buried material, was carefully scattered between the ties of the open space between the Central and Union rails. When they had finished smoothing out the roadbed, there was not a visible trace of their activities to greet a new day.

"Reckon our trap's ready for tomorrow's

big doin's, Boss," Tom Shelly said, leaning on his shovel in the moonlight. "That much dynamite will open a crater here yuh could hide a locomotive in, by grab."

Falk grinned venomously, swishing his hands outward and upward to pantomime the explosion to come.

"Everybody in a fifty-yard radius of this Golden Spike will get blasted to hashmeat," he said. "It'll be a shambles. The main thing is, we'll catch the guests of honor who have made hunted men — and bankrupt paupers, which is worse — out of the three of us. I say that justifies slaughterin' a few bystanders."

Sergeant Arkin was rubbing the pit of his stomach, his face bone-white, for nausea was touching him as he contemplated the carnage which he had helped engineer tonight. Basically Arkin was weak-charactered, but wholesale slaughter was not in him.

"I won't mind seeing Dodge and the Rio Kid and that Mexican finished," he mumbled, "but I hate to shed innocent blood."

Crade Falk twisted his head around — he was tightening his saddle latigo — his gooseberry eyes glittering with quick suspicion as he appraised the Army deserter's reaction.

"Gettin' soft, kid? Want to back out on a deal?"

Arkin caught the menace in Falk's voice, and felt like a trapped animal. He knew Falk and Shelly were through with him, and would not hesitate to back-shoot him.

"Don't get me wrong, Mr. Falk. I ain't cavin'."

Shelly, busy stowing their shovels on the burro, added a comment of his own.

"What's it to you, Sarge, if'n the Gov'nor of California and Durant and Huntington get blowed to Kingdom Come? A lot of rich fellers who begrudge their fellowmen a few measly dollars. I say, to blazes with the whole passel of 'em!"

They climbed into saddles, staring wistfully down the Union tracks toward the remote clamor of Promontory. They well knew the impossibility of joining the revelers there. It would always be that way. They were hunted men, outcasts.

"Too bad we can't see this explosion," muttered Shelly. "It'd be comfortin', when we're dodgin' the law in years to come, to think back on them kitin' sky-high."

Crade Falk gestured off toward the rocky scab-lava ridge north of the ceremony grounds.

"We'll see it," he promised. "We'll watch

the proceedin's from that hilltop yonder. And durin' the confusion after the Golden Spike sets off that blast, we'll have plenty of time to hightail to parts unknown. Nobody'll ever trace this job to any of us."

They rode off then, each conspirator silent in saddle, introspective, occupied with his own private hates and contemplation of an uncertain future. Revenge was sweet, but it was not good nourishment for a man's soul. . . .

The Rio Kid and Celestino Mireles rolled out of their bunks at dawn of May tenth, sensing the electric suspense. This day in American history had a special significance for every human being gathered to this part of Utah, and would have the same for others in years to come.

General Dodge, decked out in his full regimentals with service medals, dress saber, and glittering epaulets, disengaged himself from the milling throng of Union Pacific officials and other dignitaries and approached the Rio Kid.

"Captain Pryor," he said, "before I get too busy with all this folderol that's expected of me, I want to tell you that you are no longer responsible for my safety. I am going to commend your fine work, and

Celestino's, in my next report to President Grant. As you know, I owe you my life. But there is no longer any need for you to carry on as my bodyguard. Relax and enjoy yourself today."

The Rio Kid laughed, thanked the General, and turned back to Celestino, his eyes grave.

"Despite what Dodge just said, *amigo*, we're goin' to keep an eye on him. Falk and Shelly are probably well out of the country by now, but we can't take any chances."

Celestino fingered his sombrero chin strap, nodding.

"What I would not geev to notch my gonsights on that *diablo*, Marshal Shelly. Eet was heem who threw me eento that poisoned well, General. That I weel never forget or forgeeve."

Again on horseback, the two partners made themselves a part and yet kept themselves aloof from the great heterogeneous throng which began assembling at end-of-track. Bunting draped the coaches of the special trains which had taken the silk-hatted dignitaries to the scene. A high wind whipped dust over the polyglot mob from Promontory, hoi polloi of the West.

American flags were everywhere. Military bands played intermittently. Cavalry troops galloped here and there in formation, sabers glittering, guidons bannering.

Shortly after noon, military police formed a cordon to circle off the actual spike-driving scene. Photographers jockeyed for position, lugging their heavy plate cameras to vantage points to record the event for posterity.

The Rio Kid and Celestino, stirrup to stirrup, cruised the gathering throng, their eyes roving restlessly over the sea of heads. They knew that they would not see the outlaws they sought, but they were playing it safe.

At one o'clock on this historic day of days, the Central Pacific's diamond-stacked locomotive, *Jupiter*, steamed up from the West, its pilot beam jammed with spectators brandishing bottles of champagne and whisky to dash over the final rails for luck. From the East came the high-funneled Union Pacific engine *Number One-Sixteen*, chosen from the cavvy of Iron Horses to share the honors of the Wedding of the Rails ritual.

Crews of workmen from both camps laid the laurel and mahogany cross ties into position, under Jack Casement's honorary supervision. Then black-queued Orientals in their coolie hats, representatives from Old

Cathay from Charlie Crocker's Central Pacific track gangs, laid down one rail.

Grinning Celts from the Emerald Isle, Jack Casement's brawny graduates of Ellis Island, put the remaining rail in position and spiked it down. Only three spikes remained — those of precious metals, the sledging of which would be done by great men of the day.

In the telegraph tent, a nervous operator rechecked his sounder and key, his fuses and relays and ground connections. All of America was awaiting the message which would flash over the wires this afternoon, signaling the completion of the epochal achievement.

An elder of the Tabernacle from Brigham Young's delegation of bearded, black-hatted Latter Day Saints pronounced the invocation. The rough, shaggy mob respectfully removed their hats.

When the Almighty's blessing had been invoked, an orator mounted to the pilot beam of the U.P. locomotive and went into a flowery salutatory discourse. It reminded the Rio Kid of an address he had heard Abraham Lincoln give at the dedication of the national cemetery at Gettysburg some four years before — because it was so different.

"We are gathered here to commemorate, to dedicate, the completion of the Pacific Railway across the United States," the speaker orated. "The point of junction is one thousand, eighty-six miles west of the Missouri River, and six hundred ninety miles east of Sacramento City. Among those responsible for this meeting of the rails here at Promontory Summit, Utah, are the following celebrities . . ."

The Rio Kid, mounted on Saber, cruised the outskirts of the stirring mob, as the orator's sonorous voice began calling the roll of honor, pausing for waves of applause.

Glancing away from the crowd, toward the wind-whipped desert rise to northward, a flash of sunlight on glass or metal attracted the Rio Kid's alert eye. It was up in the scab-rock which crowned the hogback.

Curiosity — or a vague sense which caused him to move without conscious volition on his part — sent the Rio Kid's hand to his saddle-bag, to draw out a pair of Army field-glasses.

CHAPTER XV

The Golden Spike

Quickly focusing the glasses on the glint of light he had seen from the ridge summit, the Rio Kid saw something which laid a chill down his backbone.

Revealed by the powerful magnification of the binoculars was the pale, drawn face of the Army deserter, Red Arkin! The runaway spy from General Dodge's headquarters was sprawled flat amid the rocks, witnessing the joining of the rails from his lofty elevation. The flash from the insignia on his hat had betrayed him.

Heart pounding, the Rio Kid cased his glasses, loosened his Springfield in scabbard, and reined over to where Celestino Mireles sat on his black stallion.

"Arkin's hidin' in the lava bed up yonder," Pryor said briefly. "Come on. Falk and Shelly might be with him — *quien sabe?*"

Down on the tracks, the crowd was engrossed in watching silk-hatted dignitaries driving the Silver Spike, a preliminary to the climax of the ceremony, the final Golden Spike. No one noticed the two horsemen who spurred their mounts swiftly up the long rise to the north.

The Rio Kid and Celestino reined over toward the east, so as to approach Arkin's hiding place from the side. When they were within a hundred yards of the summit, on the back slope of the hogback and out of sight of the railroad, they came upon a brush-bordered defile in which three saddled horses were picketed.

"We're hitting pay dirt, General!" exclaimed Celestino, recognizing the animals which Falk and Shelly had ridden away from the kidnap shack on Promontory Point. "These ees showdown, no?"

The Rio Kid, his nerves settling down to an icy steadiness now as they invariably did when a shoot-out was in the offing, swung out of Saber's stirrups. He motioned for the Mexican youth to do likewise.

"No use riskin' our hosses," he said. He drew his Colt. "Come on, *amigo*. And watch the skyline. We don't want to be caught in an ambush here."

Leaving their horses and heading up the backbone of the ridge at a crouched dog-trot, the two justice riders suddenly heard a cry of alarm up ahead of them. The blue-clad figure of Sergeant Red Arkin appeared against the horizon above them, waving excitedly and yelling to someone behind him.

The black-coated figure of the land promoter, Crade Falk, appeared in the lava rocks behind Arkin. He was joined almost instantly by the Corinne marshal, Tom Shelly.

For an instant the bayed outlaws stared aghast at the two figures who were heading up the slope toward them, blocking their retreat toward the horses. Behind them was a wall of scab-rock which offered no refuge for a last-ditch stand. To retreat down the ridge would put them in view of the mob on the flats below.

Guns appeared in the hands of Shelly and Falk. But Red Arkin, hurling up his arms in surrender, started stumbling down the ridge toward the advancing Rio Kid and his Mexican partner.

"Hold it, Sarge!" Crade Falk snarled, cocking his gun and drawing a bead on Arkin's back. "You dirty scoundrel, yuh sold out Dodge, but yuh ain't sellin' us out!"

Arkin floundered on, panic consuming

him. With a cold laugh, Crade Falk tripped his gun hammer, drove a slug through space to catch Red Arkin between the shoulder blades.

Knocked flat by the terrific impact of the slug, Arkin rolled over on his back, his feet threshing up dust from the hill slope.

"Hold yore fire, Tom!" Falk ordered, backing up to brace his shoulders against the scab-rock ledge. "Wait till they get in easy range. We can't afford to waste a single ca'tridge."

Tom Shelly, his marshal's badge glittering in the rays of the sun, took his place against the rock wall a dozen feet from Falk. Fear had drained the color from Shelly's ragged-bearded cheeks, as he saw the Rio Kid and Celestino marching straight toward them, grim and inexorable, closing down the range which separated them.

The cold courage of their advance toward certain shoot-out put sheer terror in Shelly's soul. For that brand of iron courage was not in his own yellow make-up.

The Rio Kid, a Colt .45 jutting from either fist, spoke through the side of his mouth:

"You take Shelly, *compadre*. Falk's my meat."

A dozen feet to his right, Celestino's voice came true and sure and calm as they advanced within six-gun range:

"*Si, General.* Eef they do not surrender, Senor Shelly ees the *enemigo* I weesh to square accounts weeth."

"Halt up!" screamed Crade Falk, his iron nerve breaking. "Yuh won't take us alive!"

But the Rio Kid kept coming, and so did Celestino. Step by step, foot by foot, eyes slitted, waiting for the move which would begin this double duel to the finish.

They were abreast of Sergeant Arkin's writhing form now, as the deserter's life oozed out of the bullet-hole in his back. The Rio Kid's shadow fell briefly across the dying sergeant in passing, and Arkin whispered through the crimson foam on his lips:

"Good luck — Cap'n."

Tom Shelly was the first to break under the strain. With the inhuman shriek of a trapped animal, the marshall lunged away from the lava wall and, bracing his six-gun barrel across his left forearm, triggered a shot.

Celestino Mireles' guns exploded like cannon fire. His slugs converged on Shelly, slamming him back against the scab-rock ledge, his blood gushing from twin bulletholes on his shirt front.

Dropping to one knee, Crade Falk opened fire. Then the Rio Kid went into action, his .45s bucking and roaring against his hands. Screaming lead slammed into Falk's body and wilted the stock promoter in his tracks.

In the space of a dozen shots, the brief duel was over. At maximum six-gun range, the Rio Kid and Celestino Mireles had nailed their targets. Falk and Shelly were dead men by the time the two partners reached the lava ledge.

A gagging cry from Arkin drew them back down-slope to the Army sergeant. At first they thought he was babbling in death's last delirium:

"General Dodge — always square with me — don't want him to die down there!"

Sudden alarm touched the Rio Kid. He knelt alongside Arkin, gripping the sergeant's arm.

"Falk's dead, Arkin. General Dodge is safe now."

Arkin shook his head frantically, paroxysms of agony wracking his body, his eyes pleading up at the Rio Kid.

"Dynamite cache — under Golden Spike

— telegraph wire will — blow everyone — sky-high . . ."

A rattle gurgled in Arkin's wind pipe, and the orderly lay still, his sightless eyes still holding Rio Kid's gaze.

"Dynamite under the Golden Spike!" But Pryor yelled, "Come on, Celestino! We're probably too late — now!"

Desperation driving them, the two men raced over the summit of the ridge and slogged down the slope toward the railroad track and its crowd.

As they ran, they saw General Dodge hand a silver sledge to the distinguished Governor of California, Leland Stanford. Set in place on the mahogany Last Tie at Stanford's feet was the Last Spike, of shimmering California gold, gleaming like fire in the Utah sunlight.

Above the hubbub of the crowd, it was impossible to yell a warning. Instinct told the Rio Kid that the first stroke of Govenor Stanford's sledge, its head trailing an electric wire, would bring catastrophe to hundreds of human beings massed between the two locomotives.

As they hammered down the slope toward the telegraph tent, the Rio Kid groaned with horror as he saw Governor Stanford lift the silver sledge over his shoulder and bring it down. Nervous with the strain of the moment, Stanford's first stroke missed the Golden Spike by inches. Grinning sheepishly, he lifted the sledge for another try.

The Rio Kid skidded to a halt in front of the telegrapher's tent then. His eye caught sight of the wire which dipped into the ground, leading under the crowd to the Golden Spike.

Snatching a bowie knife from his belt sheath, he flung himself on hands and knees to the ground. With a single frantic plunge of the blade, he cut the electric wire in two.

Pandemonium went up as Stanford's down-coming sledge hit the Golden Spike, but it was not the shattering blast of a dynamite trap. It was a roar of sound from thousands of throats, blending in a paean of triumph. The locomotive whistles joined in with their ear-splitting blasts.

From the fly of the telegraph tent leaped an angry operator, staring aghast at the broken wire, the knife in the Rio Kid's hand.

"You crazy fool!" screamed the operator, his voice thin above the roar of the crowd and the locomotives' screaming whistles. "That wire's supposed to signal the sledge-hammer strokes from coast to coast!"

The Rio Kid, not unaware of the anticlimactic thing he had done, got to his feet and shoved the telegrapher aside.

"Explain later!" he yelled in the man's ear. "We'll fake those dots and dashes. No use disappointin' the whole world."

Leaping to the telegraph bench, the Rio Kid's hand fell on the hard rubber knob of the key. Three taps — and crowds in San Francisco and New York and a thousand other American cities knew that Governor Stanford was driving the Golden Spike home.

Then the Rio Kid's facile hand tapped out four letters in Morse code: "D-O-N-E."

Throughout the nation, that single word touched off wild demonstrations. The old Liberty Bell pealed out the news from Independence Hall in Philadelphia. Waiting mobs in New York's financial district heard the classic harmony of *"Te Deum"* come down the canyon of Wall Street from famous Trinity Church. In the White House at Washington, President Grant heard the clattering sounder relay the momentous tidings, and smiled in his beard.

The Rio Kid stepped out of the tent, trembling with reaction. At his feet the telegrapher squatted, sobbing like a child in his rage and disappointment. But later this afternoon, when the crowd had safely dispersed, the Rio Kid knew he would be forgiven, when they unearthed the deactivated explosive cache which lurked a few inches below the Golden Spike . . .

Celestino Mireles, with tears of emotion unashamed on his lashes, moved over beside the Rio Kid as they watched two locomotives snort black smoke from their stacks, inching forward over the new-laid rails, bells clanging, bunting rippling in the breeze.

Governor Stanford, little dreaming how close he had been to eternity, stepped off the track to stand beside General Dodge.

"You and I are witnessin' a high spot in America's winnin' of the West, Celestino," Captain Bob Pryor said in an awed whisper. "Let us be thankful we had a chance to play even a small and unsung part in this mighty undertakin'."

Celestino nodded, his throat too choked for expression of what he felt as they watched the space between the approaching locomotives narrowing. From this moment forward, the covered wagons of the Overland Trails, the stagecoaches and bullwhacker freight lines would be obsolete. The oceans were linked with steel. The westward course of empire was now complete.

Side by side, the Rio Kid and Celestino Mireles lifted their arms in grave salute, as they saw the cowcatchers meet over the Golden Spike — Iron Horses rubbing noses at the end of a long and arduous trail.